SAWATCH SKIRMISH

STONECROFT SAGA 13

B.N. RUNDELL

WOLFPACK PUBLISHING
— EST 2013 —

Sawatch Skirmish

Paperback Edition
Copyright © 2021 B.N. Rundell

Wolfpack Publishing
6032 Wheat Penny Avenue
Las Vegas, NV 89122

wolfpackpublishing.com

Paperback ISBN 978-1-64734-276-0
eBook ISBN 978-1-64734-275-3

SAWATCH SKIRMISH

DEDICATION

To my best friend and life partner, without whom I would be nothing.

1 / SPRING

The steam from the hot coffee spiraled up around his fingertips, past his moustache and curled around his nose before dissipating in the cool breeze of early morning. The rocking chair he fashioned over the winter months now squeaked a mite as he pushed back and turned to look at Cougar Woman, who sat beside him, savoring her own cup of coffee. She looked at the edge of the clearing, "The Larkspur and Chickweed are already showing color," nodding toward the purple and white flowers that usually showed their colors first.

"It's an early spring," declared Gabe, sipping at the hot brew, "but a welcome one. After that winter with its constant snows, I thought we'd never see flowers again!" He remembered the times when the snow had drifted level with the porch of their cabin, and even onto the porch that sat four feet above ground level.

"Are you still thinking about going south this summer?" asked Cougar, glancing at her tall, blonde haired and broad-shouldered man who seemed to be constantly plagued with the wanderlust of the explorer and adventurer.

"Wouldn't you like to see your family?" he asked, giving her a sidelong glance with a mischievous smile tugging at his mouth.

"Yes. My father and mother have not seen our children and it would be good for our youngsters to know them. But that is not the only reason you want to go south. You just want to see the other side of the mountains!" she answered, laughter adding a melodic tone to her words and her all-knowing smile telling even more. She knew her man and his friend were always wanting to discover and explore new country and people, and that was one of the many traits that had drawn her to him. From their first meeting, he had proven himself to be a great warrior and strong and loyal man when he and his friend, Ezra, or Black Buffalo, had fought off some attacking Blackfoot. And from that time to now, he had never ceased to fascinate and amaze her for she never thought the Creator would bless her with such a man. She had been a war leader with her tribe, the Tukkutikka Shoshone, and had resigned herself to a solitary life, until she met Gabe, or Spirit Bear, and they were immediately drawn to one another. Now they had two boys, Bobcat and Fox.

"Well, I'm ready for some warm weather, that's for sure!" declared Ezra, stepping onto the porch to join them with a hot cup of coffee in his hands. He sat down on the long bench opposite the door and scooted aside to make room for his wife, Grey Dove, to join him.

"You are always ready for warm weather," cajoled Dove, snuggling up to Ezra and smiling.

"Are they still asleep?" asked Cougar, nodding toward the cabin as she inquired about their children. Ezra, or Black Buffalo, and Dove had two youngsters, a boy, Chipmunk, and a girl, Squirrel, both close in age to the boys of Cougar and Gabe, although Chipmunk was the oldest by a little more than a year at three summers, Cougar's oldest boy was two. Dove's girl, Squirrel, and Cougar's youngest boy, Fox, were just over a year old.

Gabe and Ezra had been friends since their youth in Philadelphia and although from starkly different backgrounds, Gabe from a wealthy and socially prominent family, and Ezra the son of the pastor of the Mother Bethel African Methodist Episcopal church in Philadelphia. But the boys had been inseparable since their first foray into the woods together and had come west to explore the wilderness of the territory known as Spanish Louisiana to the west of the great Mississippi river. Although the circumstances of their leaving Philadelphia were forced on Gabe after he killed the son of a prominent family in a duel, Ezra joined him believing, as did Gabe, that this was a great opportunity to fulfill their lifelong dreams.

They had traveled down the Ohio river, crossed the Mississippi, and begun their life in the wilderness the summer of their nineteenth year. Now, almost six years later, their friendship had evolved to a brotherhood and they saw each other and their families as part of their own extended family.

"So, when we goin'?" asked Ezra, sipping at his coffee, and grinning at Gabe.

Gabe chuckled, glanced at Cougar and then to Dove, "There's still snow in the trees and the trails might be a tad muddy, but the sooner we start . . ." and shrugged his shoulders.

"Will we see my family too?" asked Dove.

"Of course!" answered Ezra, "we'll probably see them at their summer camp at our cabin there on the Popo Agie."

"I have not been there, is it far?" asked Cougar, glancing from Ezra to Gabe.

"Oh, couple weeks or so, fourteen days, thereabouts," answered Gabe, "but the mountains we want to see are about another week beyond that, or more." Their cabin was in the foothills of the Bitterroot mountains in the northern Rockies, and their initial destination would be in the Wind River mountains, far to the south. But it was the homeland of both Dove and Cougar, although they were from different bands, both were Shoshone.

Cougar looked at Dove and back to Gabe, "We should get started," and rose to go into the cabin. Gabe watched her go, a broad grin painting his face as he looked to Ezra. Dove had risen when Cougar did and both women disappeared into the cabin.

All the animals were tethered at the rail in front of the cabin, the saddle horses carried the saddles, saddle bags, and bedrolls of the adults, while the panniers and parfleches of the pack animals carried the bedrolls for the youngsters, extra blankets, additional cloth-ing, trade goods, and supplies. Over the winter, the women had fashioned a lean-to shelter from moose and elk hide, making a lighter and smaller shelter that could be carried by the pack animals without needing a travois. Once the last load was secured, the men checked each pack and rig again, and satisfied, looked to the women sitting in the rockers on the porch.

They stood, hiked the little ones onto their hips and motioned to the older boys to go to their fathers, and came down the steps to mount up. As they swung aboard their horses, they settled into the saddles and accepted the little ones as they were handed up by their men. The women would have the youngest ride with them, seated between them and the pommel of the saddle, sharing the same seat, while the men would have the older boys riding behind them.

As they lined out, Wolf, the big black wolf and their constant companion taking the point, while Gabe surrendered the lead to Ezra, riding his big bay gelding and trailing the big mule loaded with the lean-to, and Dove, aboard her buckskin gelding and trailing the other buckskin as a pack horse. Cougar followed on her strawberry roan gelding and trailing the steeldust mustang gelding, with Gabe bringing up the rear aboard his big black Andalusian stallion, Ebony, and trailing the big dapple-grey pack horse, and the spotted rump appaloosa mare with her yearling stud colt alongside.

Gabe chuckled as he looked at the parade before him, thinking they looked more like an entire village than one family, even an extended family, with their own horse herd going along. But he was glad to be out of the cabin, on the trail and headed south under a clear blue sky and cool breezes pushing down from the mountains to nudge them on their way. When they broke from the trees into the bottom of the long valley of the Big Horn river, he twisted around in his saddle for a look at the place they had called home for two years, although they weren't there for all of that time, it was still their home. The towering Bitterroot mountains with their hoary heads of white that pierced the blue of the sky behind them were a beautiful sight and he took it in, burying it deep in his memory, just in case they never returned.

A heavy sigh filled his lungs with the pine scented clear mountain air, and he turned around in his saddle to see Cougar Woman looking at the mountain valley behind them, thinking much the same as Gabe, treasuring the many memories made while living there. She smiled at Gabe and as the trail widened, Gabe kicked his black up alongside his woman, "Remembering?"

"Yes, many things, many friends."

"There will be more where we're going, and you'll see your family again."

"Yes. I am anxious to see them." She looked around, pointed with her chin to a patch of flowers showing yellow and purple with a touch of white, "It is the time of renewal, a good time to travel."

Gabe glanced at Fox, then turned to look at Bobcat, "They're growin' mighty fast, think they'll do alright?"

"It is good for them to travel, soon they will ride their own horses, perhaps those," she suggested, nodding toward the appaloosa and her yearling.

"Maybe so!" agreed Gabe, grinning.

2 / CORVETTE

They stood on the shore watching the furled sails of the three masted *Atrevida* and *Descubierta,* full of wind with streamers flying behind them, slowly fade from sight. This was not the first voyage for the Spanish Corvettes, nor was it the first venture into the gulf of California. The first voyage had been captained by Alessandro Malaspina and José de Bustamante y Guerra, but now Bustamante was a Brigadier and had arranged this voyage under the guise of a scientific expedition similar to his first voyage. He had been awakened to his need for a better fortune after Malaspina had been arrested on trumped up charges of plotting against Spain. However, this time he brought a contingent of men and horses, led by his brother-in-law, Francisco de Almeida, that he off loaded at the head of the gulf and planned to retrieve in New Orleans, after they found the gold believed to be the

Seven Cities of Cibola.

De Almeida was the first to turn away, looking to the north to the ragged edge of distant mountains far away across the flatlands at the mouth of the Colorado River. He reviewed in his mind just as his second, Diego Gomez stepped beside him, "So, we go north to the Brazos de la Miraflores?"

Francisco huffed, "It is known as the Gila River."

"But your map has the Brazos name," he reminded his friend and the leader of the band of explorers.

"Si. We follow the Colorado to the Gila, maybe three, four days away, then we follow the Gila to the headwaters."

"And then?" asked the curious Diego, removing his doublet jacket as he looked at the blazing sun, then to the other men, lounging on the packs and gear just off-loaded from the ship. There were only a half-dozen horses, twelve pack mules, and a total of thirty men for the expedition to the interior of New Spain, also known as Spanish Louisiana, the territory gained from France.

"Overland to the Rio Bravo del Norte. We follow that river north into a wide basin, continue north across some mountains to another river that flows from the north and to the east. A smaller river called the Arkansa."

"And that is where we find Quivira?"

Francisco scowled at his number two, "Perhaps."

Although it was not a military expedition, the band assumed ranks as appointed by the brigadier aboard ship. Francisco de Almeida, Capitan, Diego Gomez, Lieutenant, Jorge Alvares, Miguel Corte-Real, Antonio De Noli, and Duarte Fernandes, Sergeants. Each sergeant had six men under him and three pack mules for their gear and tools. The Capitan, Lieutenant, and Sergeants rode the horses while the rest of the men walked beside the mules. It would be a long journey, estimated to be at least six to eight weeks to their destination on the east side of the long range of mountains known as the Sawatch range of the Rocky Mountains and the headwaters of the Arkansa river.

Diego looked at Francisco, glanced back at the men who had already taken count of the number of horses and men, then asked Francisco, "The men are already asking about horses. Did your brother-in-law tell you about the mission and if there were more horses?"

"Si. There is a mission at the confluence of rivers, and he was certain there would be horses."

"I will let them know."

"When they pack the mules, tell the men to keep their rifles. There are some natives all along our route and not all will be friendly."

"Si, mi Capitan," stated Diego as he turned away and stalked to the men, motioning them to their feet and began barking orders.

After four days on the trail, the men had settled into a routine, the mules became more docile and the travel became mundane. After most of a year aboard ship, most were glad to be on solid ground and in a new country. The terrain was not unlike their homeland, mostly flat, dry except along the river banks, and humid with an unrelenting sun always bearing down on them. Most of the men had some form of head gear that offered shade for their face and neck, but the usual head scarf had been tucked away and their doublet jackets adorned the mules. Some tried to stuff their rifles into the packs but were quickly admonished by the sergeants and submitted to carrying their weapons.

They sighted the ruins of an adobe structure as they neared the confluence of the Colorado and the Gila rivers. Francisco rode close to the deteriorated walls, and when Diego came alongside, he pointed, "That was a mission. That," pointing to the northern end of the ruins, "was the altar."

"Is this the mission we were to find horses?" asked Diego.

"This was the Mission San Pedro y San Pablo. I was told it was a mission to the Quechan Indians and would have access to the Indian horses."

Diego grunted, shaking his head, "If the Quechan did this, I do not think they will give us any horses."

"No, but they might be willing to trade. That is why

we have so many trade goods," suggested Francisco, nodding across the river to what appeared to be a village of dome shaped structures. They saw one man on the far bank beside some trees that was watching them, and Francisco lifted his hand to wave at the man, causing him to disappear into the trees.

They crossed the Colorado River after pushing through the thick Palo Verde and mesquite trees. It was an easy crossing, the lazy river, though deep, was refreshing to both man and beast. Once across, they followed the north bank of the Gila, having to parallel the river away from the thickets and grease wood brush. Some of the trees looked like smoke with the grey bark and wispy branches and the further they strayed from the water, the desert lands seemed to grab at them with ocotillo and cholla cactus.

They stopped and Francisco turned to the other men that sat horseback, "Find the trade goods, sort out some cloth, mirrors, knives, beads, and maybe a rifle or two with powder and such. Diego and I will go to the village to arrange a trade." He looked at the four men, nodded to Antonio de Noli, "You, station some of the men, rifles ready but out of sight, in the trees, there," pointing to the edge of the trees that bordered the river. He looked at another sergeant, Jorge Alvares, "You, have two men picket the mules and hide the packs."

As the men stepped to their duties, Francisco

motioned to Diego and the two men started to the village. It was a large village with almost a hundred lodges, several warriors holding lances stood before the trail that led into the village and stopped the two as they rode near. Francisco lifted a hand and spoke, *"Venimos a comerciar!"* The warriors looked from one to another until one man stepped forward and answered in Spanish, "What is it you want to trade from our people?"

"We need horses and food. We have many goods to trade."

"I will tell our people. If they want to trade, they will come to your camp," stated the speaker, turning away to dismiss the visitors. The other warriors turned and followed the speaker, none looking back at the two men that sat horseback.

Francisco looked at Diego, "Friendly, aren't they?"

Diego grunted, reined his horse around to return to their camp and prepare for the trade. When they returned, their men had been stationed as ordered, but Francisco asked all the men to come near and he explained what would happen. "I do not know how many will come, but two men must always be near, rifles ready, and two others near the packs with the trade goods. Do not shoot unless they attack! There are many more of them than we can take, so be cautious."

In less than an hour, a large contingent of the natives, some leading horses, others riding, the men wore woven breechcloths, the women skirts of willow bark strips. Most wore some form of jewelry made from shells and beads, but they were excited about the trade beads of bright colors offered by the Spaniards. Many came to the camp of the Spaniards and trading began. Several of the Quechan had learned Spanish from the priests at the mission and talk ensued between the traders and the natives, and trade was brisk and profitable for the Spaniards, but the natives were pleased with their new goods as well.

When the trade was finished, the Spaniards had garnered twelve horses and a good supply of smoked fish. The load of trade goods was considerably lighter, lessened by beads, metal mirrors, and three rifles with powder and lead. "Maybe we can find more horses at another village," offered Diego.

"Si, until then, the men will have to alternate riding and walking, but it will make our travel faster. They should be happier now," declared Francisco. He often had difficulty showing any concern or compassion for the men, believing himself to be of noble birth and above such behavior and grumbling of the commoners.

"We will have to keep a close watch on the men if we come to another village, one of those Quechan offered his woman to Antonio for a rifle, but . . ."

Francisco turned to scowl at Diego, "I will have none of that. You can let the men know I will not hesitate to use this," placing his hand on the butt of his pistol that protruded above his sash, "if they disobey me!"

"Si, mi Capitan! I will let them know," answered Diego, turning his head away to hide his scowl. He shook his head slightly as he went to the men to explain about the camp and more. As he walked, he reminded himself of the anticipated wealth that would be gained if their expedition was successful, and had the passing thought that if the Capitan had an accident, well, who would know?

3 / CAMP

"We're campin' here!" declared Ezra, twisting in his seat to look at the others as they came into the grassy flat beside the river. They had been traveling for eight days, covering a great distance on mountain trails. After taking a southbound trail that followed the middle fork of the three forks that fed the Missouri River, they rode through a wide gorge and broke into the open when the trail led them to the confluence of two smaller rivers that formed the middle fork. The wide grassy flat lay below the timbered shoulder of the foothills that butted together to form a broad mesa that lay on the south flanks of granite tipped mountains of the Absaroka range. It was a wild and challenging but beautiful country, full of game and strange geologic wonders. They knew they were coming into the land of many waters and would soon see the many geysers and hot springs that made this amazing land.

"I am ready for a few days rest," declared Cougar Woman, pronouncing her will for the next few days.

Gabe looked at her with lifted eyebrows, then grinned, "I reckon we could use some rest and maybe some fresh meat. From the looks of those streams yonder," pointing with his chin to the confluence of streams, "Ezra'll prob'ly be doin' his best to get us some fish!"

"You got that right! I'm hankerin' for somethin' that doesn't taste like smoke!" answered Ezra as he swung down from his big bay and helping Chipmunk to the ground. He walked to the side of Dove's buckskin and reached up to take Squirrel from her mother. Dove slipped to the ground and stretched. Without a glance to the others, she strode to the stream and bellied down beside the cold clear water and with her face in the water, drank deeply. She sat up, water dripping from her chin and smiling, looking around, and turned to Cougar Woman, "Yes! It is time we rested!"

Gabe grinned, looked to Ezra, "And there you have it! We have been told! Rest it is!"

Gabe swung his leg over Ebony's neck, slipped to the ground and reached up for Bobcat, set him on his hip and went to Cougar Woman to take Fox, and put both boys on the ground in the deep grass.

The river made a dog-leg bend away from the trees, making a broad grass covered peninsula, but Gabe led the big grey packhorse and the steeldust mustang to the edge of the trees to drop the packs and start shaping up their camp. Ezra followed, leading the mule and the buckskin pack horse. They had dropped the reins on their horses to ground tie the animals, letting them snatch mouthfuls of grass. Once the packs were stacked, the men rubbed down the animals with dry grass, and let them join the appaloosa mare and her colt at river's edge for a deep drink of cold water.

Their routine of setting up camp had become a standard ritual, each one stepping to their duties, including the older children fetching close-in firewood. Before long, the fire ring had been set, the fire started, and the horses picketed. While Ezra set-off to get some fish for their supper, Gabe and Wolf started to the crest of shoulder that offered a view of the country side and Gabe's habit was to have a look-see to know what was near. Wolf led the way as they wound through the timber, paused at a slight shoulder, but was motioned on by Gabe. Once atop the crest, he found a bald knob with a large boulder that offered a good promontory and they soon lay stretched out, side by side, as Gabe unlimbered his brass telescope to view the area. Wolf watched, tongue lolling after the climb, then lay his head between his paws to wait for his friend. To the east, the green valley stretched like a crooked arrow pointing to the distant horizon marked by a long ridge with unremarkable features. On the south, the direction they would travel, the river cut a canyon at the edge of a wide timber covered mesa, but the trail stayed atop the flat and would take them to the far basin with alkali painted flats and sulfurous geysers. Directly across from the camp, the edge of the wide mesa was marked by steep rimrock lined talus slopes that caved away to the river bottom. The west canyon held the trail that brought them to their camp.

He moved the scope back to the east, looking at a white mound with a thin pillar of steam rising to dissipate into the thin mountain air. One of the many hot springs, marked by the bright orange colored scars atop the mound showing the source of the mineral laden water. Below the mound and closer in, a couple of pools, one rust colored, the other deep azure blue, showed other smaller springs. Near the river, a small herd of big-horn sheep were taking their evening drink while the lambs cavorted in the grass. Gabe counted three rams, five ewes, and five lambs. The herd ram stood proudly watching his family, the curls of his horns making a full circle and more. The other rams were sparring with one another, while the ewes drank and munched on the deep green grass.

Beyond the big-horns, probably two hundred yards, the river twisted back on itself and a sizable moose stood knee deep in the water, greenery hanging from his jowls as he munched contentedly. None of the animals showed any concern nor alerted of any danger or unwelcome visitors. Gabe swung his scope back to the south, scanning the trail and the flats that held the south bound trail. He spotted what he guessed to be a herd of elk, but they were too far off to tell for sure before they filed into the black timber. One last scan of the entire area satisfied his curiosity and concern, and he stuffed the scope back in its case and rolled to his side to look at Wolf who appeared to be asleep. Gabe rubbed behind his ears, and the big beast moaned in enjoyment, opened his eyes to look at his friend as Gabe said, "Let's go back down, shall we, boy?" and sat up.

Gabe dug in his heels as they descended the steep slope, sliding on his rump and reaching back to keep from falling. Wolf loped down without difficulty, stopped and with his head cocked to the side, looked back at Gabe with an expression that told of his wonderment at the awkward man that followed. When they walked into camp, Gabe saw the coffeepot dancing on the flat rock beside the flames and quickly snatched up a cup and poured himself some, watching it boil up as it came from the spout. He sat down beside Wolf and watched the women as they dutifully prepared the meal of potatoes, carrots, and greens. The vegetables would be cooked whenever Ezra returned with his catch, which would be the main dish for the meal.

Gabe looked up the stream, didn't see Ezra, and sat his now empty cup on the rock and said, "We'll go check on him, see if we can hurry him up. I'm gettin' hungry!" The women nodded, paying more attention to the scampering, and playing youngsters than Gabe and Wolf. Gabe glanced at Wolf, then to the river, and stepped to get his rifle before leaving. He always had his over/under Bailes double-barreled pistol in his belt, but he thought his Ferguson rifle might come in handy. He shook his head as he grinned, thinking, *Can never be too careful!*

He knew Ezra had taken to the stream that came from the south, the hot mineral springs to the east would taint the water and the fish would shy away from the warmer stream. Determined to have a good catch for supper, Ezra opted for the stream that showed more whitewater and followed the shoulder of the big mesa. Gabe waded across the stream by the camp and followed the trail that showed Ezra's tracks. The trail hugged the east bank of the cascading stream, the narrow bank marked by fallen timber and high water from spring run-off. A wider trail lay off the bank and rose into the black timber, it was the trail they would follow, but it was too far from the stream and Ezra's tracks stayed on the narrow stream-side trail. A wide bend hid the course of the stream and the cascading waters rumbled, the sounds bouncing off the steep canyon walls.

As the trail widened where it made the bend, Wolf paused, growling, and looking through the trees. Gabe asked, "What is it boy?" in a whisper, dropping to one knee beside the beast. He peered through the trees, thought he saw movement and started forward, earing back the hammer on his rifle. A few steps further and Gabe saw Ezra backing down the trail, watching something beyond him, his pistol in his hand and arms outstretched at his sides. Gabe stepped closer, spoke to Ezra, "What's wrong? What is it?"

"Grizz! Big 'un!" replied Ezra, cautiously stepping backwards, closer to Gabe. Wolf started forward, head down, teeth showing, a low rumbling growl coming from deep in his chest.

Gabe spoke to Wolf, "Easy boy, easy," and walked beside the wolf, picking his steps as he lifted the rifle to his shoulder, keeping the muzzle down.

"I'm behind you, I'll be on your left. Keep coming," directed Gabe, speaking softly.

"I threw him my fish, he seems satisfied, but he keeps lookin' at me like I'm next on his menu!" explained Ezra. "All I have is my pistol and that would just make him mad!"

"Ummhmm," agreed Gabe.

Ezra was closer, almost to Gabe's side, but refused to take his eyes off the big bear. He took another step, stumbled on a rock, and almost fell, but caught his balance. The bear rose up on his hind feet, growled a roar that filled the canyon and bounced back. He cocked his head to the side, snapped his jaws repeatedly, showing a gaping maw that was big enough to take Gabe's head in one bite. The big bruin slapped at the air before him, showing massive paws and claws twice as long as Gabe's fingers. The huge brown beast stood over eight feet tall, closer to nine, and took two steps forward, threatening the men before him.

Wolf stepped before Gabe, growling and snarling, making the bear look down. The grizzly snapped his jaws, looked at the wolf, slapped the air before him and dropped to all fours, glaring at Wolf. Gabe said, "Easy boy, easy. Let's back outta here, c'mon now. He's too big for us!"

Gabe took a tentative step back, Ezra already behind him, but lifted his rifle as he moved. He stepped back again, called to Wolf, "C'mon boy, let's go," and the wolf growled, stepped back beside Gabe and the three eased their way into the trees. The big bear looked down at the remaining fish and dropped to his belly to enjoy his feast, no longer concerned by the intruders to his domain.

Once behind the trees, the men turned and started quick stepping down the trail, looking over their shoulder often, but making time with Wolf at their side. When they were more than a hundred yards away from the bear, they slowed, looked back up the trail and seeing no movement, Gabe said, "Guess he liked your fish! But now, what are we having for supper?"

"Would you believe smoked venison?" answered Ezra.

4 / FISH

Just before first light, Wolf woke Gabe with a low rumbling growl as he came to his feet beside the sleeping form. They were in the lean-to shelter, enclosed on all sides, but Gabe and Wolf lay at the edge and he rolled to the side to slowly lift the edge of the hide covering. He looked about the camp as far as he could see, noticed Ebony standing alert with head lifted and ears forward. Gabe slowly moved the blankets aside, grabbed his Ferguson rifle and slipped under the lifted cover, Wolf behind him. The lean-to was just inside the tree line and the sloping river bank shone in the moonlight, and a shadow moved near water's edge. Gabe was in the shadow of a tall ponderosa, not easily seen and Wolf leaned against the man's leg, allowing Gabe to feel the almost silent growl.

He searched the wide grassy peninsula, the brush beside the water, and the lower end of the grassy flat.

The shadowy darkness at river's edge moved and Gabe brought up the Ferguson. He thought of their run-in with the Grizzly and the size of the shadow gave cause for caution. He breathed easy, unmoving, watching, and waiting for the shadow to show itself against the lighter moonlit grassy flat. Ezra had slipped out the other side of the cover, whispered, "What is it?"

"Dunno," whispered Gabe without taking his eyes off the shadow. With the smell of horses in the air he knew they would be a temptation for a hungry grizzly that had enjoyed his appetizer of fish, but it certainly had not satisfied the ravenous appetite of the largest predator in the mountains. Yet the horses were not frightened, and the smell of bear would alert both Ebony and the Mule, but the mule stood hipshot, unmoving and snoozing. Ebony still watched, nostrils flaring, eyes wide and ears pointing.

Gabe focused on the unmoving shadows that appeared to be darker, thicker, more so than the wispy willows that usually dipped in the rushing water. The shadow moved, a black silhouette that was bigger than a horse, when it seemed to separate and a smaller shadow trotted quickly into the tall grass, as Gabe and Ezra breathed in relief. The big ears and long legs were the giveaway, a gangly moose calf had left its mother by the river and romped playfully in the tall grass below the lean-to. Gabe looked at Ezra, saw the white teeth show in the darkness and heard his throaty chuckle as he whispered, "That would be good eatin' if she didn't have a calf!" he declared quietly.

Gabe answered with a low chuckle, lowering his Ferguson to stand the butt on his foot and lean it against his body. He looked at the sky, saw the first light of grey morning chasing the darkness from the sky as the lanterns of the night snuffed out their lights. "I'm goin' up yonder," stated Gabe, nodding to the hill behind the camp. It was his habit to spend the early hours of the day with his Lord in a time of thanksgiving and prayer.

"I'm goin' thataway!" answered Ezra, following his own inclination and habit just like Gabe's. Although he had established his routine well before Gabe, Ezra was always encouraged to see his friend follow the practice.

When they returned from the hilltops, Cougar and Dove had the fire going and breakfast cooking. The women had found some duck eggs by the stream, sliced some cattail shoots and roots and onions, and had the batch cooking over the flames. The coffeepot sat on the flat rock beckoning to the men and they eagerly responded, sipping the hot coffee as they held the steaming cups at their chins.

Dove looked at Ezra, "Are you going to get us some fish today?"

Ezra grinned, "Yes, of course! If you want fish, I'll

get you fish. I had some for you yesterday but that ol' grizz was hungrier than I was, and he won out."

"No fighting of grizzly bears today!" admonished Dove, smiling at her man, "but don't give away my fish!"

"Yes! We would like some fish for our meal tonite!" added Cougar Woman, trying to maintain a stern expression.

Gabe added, "Yeah, fisherman! What's the deal? Am I gonna hafta show you how to fish?"

Ezra shook his head, chuckling, glancing from one to the other, "Yassuh boss, Yassuh missus, whats eveh you say missy. This ol' slave gonna get you some fish rightaway!"

Everyone laughed at Ezra's mimicking of a slave, each one knowing slavery wasn't a laughing matter, but Ezra's characterization was funny, and they couldn't help themselves. Although the women had never seen slavery among white civilization and had no idea of the manner portrayed by Ezra, they had seen slavery first-hand among the different tribes of the wilderness and knew that many captives were poorly treated and killed even after living a life of slavery for years.

"Well, I'll come along to protect you from the bears, and if you don't get us enough fish, maybe I can get us some meat of a different kind," added Gabe.

Ezra looked at Gabe and at the stream, "What'chu

think? Upstream or down?"

"Upstream there's a couple hot pots and steamers, so, prob'ly downstream."

They started off together, walking below the confluence of the streams and working their way past the willows, peeking in between the brush whenever possible for a good fishing hole. The river made a dogleg bent back toward the tall rocky butte on the far side of the stream that stood like a solitary fortress, dead snags showing a long-ago fire and rocky talus at the shoulder with scattered fir trees clinging to the steep slope. The base of the butte was skirted with a wide band of spruce and ponderosa before the long grassy flat that led to the river. Where Gabe and Ezra walked the willows had given way to grass and the bend in the river afforded an undercut bank, a great hidey hole for trout.

Ezra pointed to the deep pool, mouthed the words, "I'll try here!" and sat down to put a couple of fresh-caught grasshoppers on the hook. Gabe looked around, saw a couple gnarly pines on a slight knoll that offered shade and deep grass that beckoned him and with a hand signal to Wolf, the two walked to the shade and stretched out. Gabe pushed his hat over his eyes, lay his rifle at his side, the barrel in the crook of his arm. With a glance at Wolf who was stretched out but with his head lifted to watch Ezra by the river, he closed his eyes for a mid-morning snooze.

Ezra had stretched out on his belly, the willow fishing pole extended over the edge of the bank, and the line floating toward the round shoulder of grass. Within just a few moments, the grasshopper was gobbled up and the hook set as he rolled to his side and brought the big cut-throat trout into the grass. He sat up, took the fish off the hook and conked its head with a bigger stick, tossed it into the grass and with most of the grasshopper still on the hook, he tossed it back in the water. Gabe had been peeking through slit eyes from under the brim of his hat and grinned at the fisherman enjoying himself.

As Ezra continued his foray into a fisherman's dream, he glanced up to see the cow moose on the far bank, stepping into the shallow water and dropping her head into the ripples. The calf had been running around and soon dropped to his belly while watching his mother munch on the greens from the shallow eddy at stream's edge. Ezra grinned, enjoying the fishing, watching the moose, and the magnificent scenery all around. It was a beautiful morning, clear blue sky, bright sunshine, not a cloud in the sky, and the fish were fighting over his bait, he was happy. He looked at his catch, counted eight trout, both cut-throat and browns, and impaled on his forked willow hanger, and none less than fifteen inches. He grinned, shook his head, muttered to himself, *Maybe three or four more should do it.*

But a patch of brown at the edge of the willows on the far bank caught his eye. He scowled, shaded his eyes, and leaned forward, watching. He was afraid of what he saw, shaking his head in unbelief, *It's that blasted grizz!* Movement closer in caught his attention and he saw the long-legged cow moose splash from the water, eyes on her calf that lay in the grass. With a glance to the grizzly, she nudged her calf, almost rolling him over, and as the gangly youngster struggled to his feet, she pushed him toward the water. She looked back at the bruin who was starting to lumber toward her, his eyes on the tender calf, and with another shove, the two went into the water.

Ezra jumped to his feet, watching the moose splash across the shallow river, white water splashing high as she dropped her bulbous nose to push her calf who was struggling in the rushing stream. Although it wasn't deep for her long legs, it was almost to the belly of the calf, but she pushed him along as he protested with a bleet and blubber as his nose dipped into the water. He shook his head as he lifted it up, splashing his way to the grassy bank.

The grizzly neared the edge of the far bank, saw his prey splashing through the current and without missing a step, the big brown beast stretched out and leaped into the water, splashing down about eight feet from the bank. His big paws, each the size of a frying pan, splashed water high, every step sending water flying. His massive form seemed to part the water as his jaw hung open, snarling and growling, his long teeth and lolling tongue flashing with every snap of his jaw.

For just a moment, Ezra was frozen in place, but just until the bear hit the water. He turned to look toward Gabe, then screamed, "BEAR! BEAR!" and turned to flee. He snatched up the willow hanger with the fish and started towards Gabe, just as the moose lunged from the water, almost knocking him down. He fell to his knees, pushed against the flank of the moose to keep her from stepping on him, and jumped to his feet. He glanced back to see the bear nearing the bank and started to run.

Gabe and Wolf heard Ezra's shout and came to their feet. In an instant, Gabe took in the scene and started at a trot toward Ezra, Wolf running ahead. As Ezra stumbled through the deep grass, Wolf came near, saw the cow moose and her calf running toward the trees, and looked at Ezra, as if asking him *What?* But the smell of bear filled his nostrils and he stepped aside to see the big grizzly coming from the water, then heard Gabe shout from behind him. "The fish! Give him the fish!"

Ezra didn't miss a step as he shouted back, "NO!" and kept running.

Wolf saw the bear hump his back and start to run. His eyes were no longer on the calf moose, but on Ezra, probably smelling the fish. Wolf stood his ground, bared his teeth, and growled, snarling, and snapping his jaws. He glared at the bear, now coming at a run, then glanced at the back of Ezra as he made for the trees, looked back at the bear, and heard Gabe shout, "Wolf, C'mere!, and he twisted around and with a long lunge, headed for his friends, his back to the bear.

Ezra made it to Gabe's side, but didn't slow down as he ran past, Gabe glaring at him as he caught his stride and headed for the trees. Gabe looked at the bear, hollered at Ezra, "LEAVE THE FISH!" and heard another, "NO!" shouted over Ezra's shoulder. Gabe looked at the charging grizzly, lifted his rifle, thought better of it, and snatched his pistol, cocking it as he brought it up and fired over the head of the charging bear, hoping to distract it from his charge. But, as he suspected, a big grizzly is not easily discouraged, the sound of the shot and the bullet whistling by his head mattered little enough and Gabe turned and ran for the trees.

Both Gabe and Ezra knew they would never outrun a grizzly, but if they could just make it up a good-sized tree, maybe they could get by without killing him. As Gabe stretched out his long legs, he heard Ezra, "Here! Up here!" and saw his friend scampering up a big ponderosa. Gabe looked for another, slipping his rifle over his shoulder to hang from the sling at his back, and spotted another big ponderosa and whipped around to the back side, leaped high for the lowest branch, and pulled himself up. The sticky sap giving his feet traction and within seconds he was well off the ground, but the bear was stretching out, reaching up as high as he could and his massive paw swiped at Gabe's moccasin, missing it by inches.

Gabe looked at Ezra, about thirty feet away and higher in his tree than Gabe, "Why's he after me? You got the fish!"

"You were closer!" answered Ezra.

"Where's Wolf?"

"He's smarter than we are, he's prob'ly gone to the camp for the women to protect him!"

"Why didn't you give him the fish?"

"He had his fish yesterday! I ain't givin' him anymore!"

"You might be eatin' 'em raw if he don't go away!" grumbled Gabe.

5 / GEYSERS

"You can come down now!" called Cougar Woman as she stood beneath the ponderosa, Wolf at her side, looking up at the strange breed of tree dwellers.

Gabe looked down at Cougar, glanced over to Ezra, and said to his life's partner, "You sure that grizz is gone?"

"We saw him fishing down at the river, looks like he was catching a few!"

Gabe shook his head, laughing, as he made his way from branch to branch and dropped to the ground. Ezra had dropped his catch and followed them to the ground and looked over at Gabe, "See there! He's gone and we still have our fish!"

"Dried out and in need of cleaning. Maybe they'll still be edible, but you'd have saved us a lot of trouble if you just gave 'em up!" declared Gabe, shaking his head as he put his arm around Cougar Woman's waist as they started back to camp.

"You could have just shot him too!" grumbled Ezra.

"One shot from this rifle would have just made him mad! And your fishing pole sure wouldn't have stopped him!"

Cougar laughed at the men, laid her rifle across her shoulder, barrel forward, and added, "Well, Dove has some hot biscuits waiting, so you won't go hungry."

It was by the dim grey light of early morning that the family stretched out on the trail south. Gabe and Cougar led the way, familiar country for Cougar Woman for it was the summer territory of the Tukkutikka band of the Shoshone and they hoped to find the encampment soon. The feeder river that merged with the middle fork cut its way through the edge of the high bluff, carving a deep canyon below the rimrock edge of the mountain. The trail rode the flat mesa to the east of the river, winding its way through the intermittent timber of spruce, fir, and pine. Within an hour they broke from the trees into a veritable waste land of dead snags, alkali flats, and intermittent pools of hot springs that showed a variety of colors from azure blue to deep rust. The white minerals that covered the flats and low knobs shone stark against the deep black of the distant timber. The morning sun bounced hot rays off the chalky terrain, forcing the riders to shade their eyes from the glare. The stench of sulfurous waters masked the usual fresh pine scent of the mountains.

Cougar Woman pointed them in a direct route across the dry flat, motioning to the greenery beside the river as it came from the trees. She led them on a straight south route, preferring the shade of the trees to the glare of the flats. After rounding a talus sloped bluff, the trail rode the east bank of the river while the west bank showed a wide pool of turquoise blue waters surrounded by yellow and orange mineral build-up at water's edge. The overflow from the deep spring spread the stinking minerals across the white slopes, marring the wasteland of desolation.

They left the river's edge and went to the trees, enjoying the respite from the sulfurous stench replaced by the sweet smell of pines. Gabe breathed deep, filling his lungs with the refreshing air, and looked at Cougar Woman as she laughed at him. "The biggest geyser is just ahead." She nodded to Bobcat, "I think he will be surprised to see such a wonder."

"What wonder, mother?" asked the boy. Gabe twisted around to look at the usually silent boy, frowned, and glanced to Cougar, "Listen to him, would'ja?"

Bobcat frowned at his father, looked to his mother as he raised his eyebrows in question. Cougar smiled and answered, "A place where a big fountain of water shoots straight up out of the ground and makes a big noise!"

"Why?"

"Because that's the way the Creator made it."

"Oh," answered the boy, leaning his head against his father's back and tucking his fingers in Gabe's belt.

As they wound their way through the timber, following a well-used game trail, they made good time. It was late morning when they neared the edge of the trees, and the rumbling from deep within the ground began. The horses became skittish, careful of each step, looking at the ground and feeling the vibration beneath their feet. The riders reached down to stroke the horse's necks, talking to them, and encouraging them to keep moving. Gabe slid to the ground, motioned the others to do the same, and walk beside the head of their mounts. The pack animals watched the others and were stilled by the example of the saddle horses with the riders at their sides. Each one kept a tight grip on the reins, holding close to the bridles and continually touching and talking to the horses.

"If we hurry, we'll see the geyser!" declared Cougar, starting to walk faster, leaning side to side to see around the trees and looking to the flats before them.

They broke from the trees just as the big geyser began to boil from the ground. The water was clear, a slight aquamarine color, and it boiled bigger and bigger. The ground trembled, the skittish horses wide-eyed, pulling at their leads, and stepping sideways, fearful of the unknown tremors and strange noises. The tower of steam preceded the waterspout and as the geyser began to climb higher and higher, the splatter of water and the hiss of the steam added to the pandemonium. The monster from the deep hissed and spat, rising ever higher, splattering water, and shooting steam, until it reached its apex over two hundred feet high! Everyone stood, mouths agape, eyes wide, even the horses watched, mesmerized by the sight. As it continued to spew, the wonder paled, and the gaze of the observers began to take in the nearby sights including the reaction of the children.

Gabe nodded toward Bobcat, who was pointing with pudgy fingers, bright eyed and smiling. He looked at his mother, laughing and pointing, "Wonder!" he declared. Cougar Woman smiled, nodding, and looked at Fox, astraddle of her hip with his head leaning against her breast and eyes closed in sleep. She looked to Dove's little ones who were reacting in much the same way, Chipmunk staring stoically as if it was nothing to be excited about, but Squirrel was giggling and pointing.

As the geyser began to sputter and lessen, the tower of water lowering, the band of travelers led the horses around the flat, well-away from the water, and headed to the trees. As the horses became calm, everyone mounted up and followed Cougar into the trees. After a short break for a mid-day meal and some rest for the animals, they were once again on the trail south. The trail was an easy one, the trees sparse, and they often rode side by side. They stayed atop a wide mesa that overlooked a big lake that lay in the bottom of the timbered basin. "My people call that Shoshone Lake," declared Cougar as she pointed out the big cobalt blue body of water. "Our trail will take us below that lake and to the far side of the lower lake, there," pointing to a more distant smaller lake.

Gabe glanced at the sun, guessed the time remaining and the distance to the smaller lake, "That looks to be a good place to camp for the night." With another look to the sky, he saw some dark clouds behind them to the north, but they were far away and not of special concern. The rest of the sky was clear, and the spring sun was warm on their backs, making for a pleasant day's travel.

"The little ones are tired and sleeping," stated Cougar, smiling as she pointed with her chin to Bobcat, leaning his cheek against his father's back and sleeping, rocking with the steady gait of the horse.

"Yeah, but they'll prob'ly be wide awake and full of mischief 'bout the time we stop for camp!" answered Gabe. He glanced back at Ezra and Dove, saw Ezra had put Chipmunk in the seat in front of him, and they were chattering on as Ezra pointed out different trees, plants, and animals as he taught his son in the wilderness classroom. Squirrel was leaning back against her mother's breasts, sound asleep.

They crossed the narrow river that flowed from Shoshone Lake into the smaller lake at a wide, shallow crossing about a mile and a half above the small lake, the water bringing the children wide awake and when the horses stopped to roll their hides and shake off the water, the little ones held tight, laughing and enjoying the shaking. It was just a little over three miles around the bend of the lake to the campsite selected by Cougar, a site her people had used before. It was at the edge of some tall ponderosa, back from water's edge, but overlooking the pristine waters of the mountain lake. Everyone was tired and as the women fixed the meal, the men tended to the horses and the lean-to and as dusk dropped the curtain of darkness, they crawled into their blankets for a good night's rest.

6 / CLOUDBURST

Wolf was restless as he crawled under the overhang of the lean-to, Gabe stirred and rolled to his side to lift the flap enough to look into the moonlit night. Wolf trotted into the trees making Gabe think his furry friend was hearing the call of the wild from some female lobo in the night. As he rolled to his side to face Cougar, a little balled up fist connected with his nose reminding him that Fox and Bobcat were both lying between them. He chuckled to himself and grinned as he sought refuge in slumber. The distant thunder lulled him to sleep.

When Gabe felt Wolf's cold nose on his neck, he pulled away, scowling at the black wolf, but reached out to run his hand through the scruff of his friend's neck, whispering to him, "Alright, alright, I'm coming." Gabe glanced to Cougar, saw the white of her teeth showing her smile and whispered, "We're goin' to the hilltop." Cougar nodded, glanced at the boys, and watched her man crawl from the shelter.

Gabe stood and stretched, looking at the fading stars, already tucking themselves away against the coming daylight, then reached down to stroke Wolf, motioning him to lead the way to a likely spot for morning prayer. As they started away from the camp, Gabe glanced back to see Ezra crawling from under the hide cover and wave as Gabe and Wolf disappeared into the trees. Behind their camp a long timbered slope led to the crest of a rugged ridge with a steep drop-off on the far side to a meandering creek that carried runoff water from both the ridge and a cluster of mountains further south.

Not wanting to climb all the way to the top of the ridge, Gabe chose a bald knob of a shoulder that offered a view of the lake and the southern trail. The sunrise would make a long shadow of the higher butte, but the trees offered a wind break. He took a seat on a grassy point, Wolf sat beside him. Gabe breathed deep, glancing to the east expecting to see the first light of early morning, but a distant stab of lightning startled him. He had heard the low rumble of thunder in the night, but thought little of it, the macabre fingers of blue knifing into the trees giving a stark reminder. He opened the pages of his Bible and began to read but was continually distracted with the lightning and thunder. He saw another jagged white bolt against the dark clouds, counted until he heard the thunder, and calculated the storm to be at least ten to fifteen miles away, affording ample time to make any preparations necessary. If the storm didn't veer off some other direction, they would not be traveling this day.

Wolf came to his feet, looking back toward their camp as he whimpered. As Gabe frowned, he felt a hollowness in his gut, the emptiness that gives a sense of foreboding. He shook his head, wanting to focus on his time of prayer, believing the forces that be were preventing his concentration, but the feeling would not leave. He muttered a quick prayer, glanced to the distant storm in the east, and rose to return to camp. He knew Ezra, with his Gaelic heritage and his mother's history with the Druids, had an uncanny ability, or sense of impending danger that had warned them many times of trouble to avoid, but Gabe's own sense of precognition was nothing in comparison to his friend's. A quick glance heavenward showed the grey canopy promising a soon sunrise.

Wolf led the way back to camp and Gabe was surprised to see the activity in camp. The children were scampering about, and Dove was busy at the fire, Ezra apparently still on the mountain. Gabe stepped to the shelter, pushed the hide cover aside expecting to see Cougar, but the cover held nothing but rumpled blankets. He stood and turned to Dove, "Where's Cougar?"

"She left early to get some fresh meat before the storm comes," explained Dove, adding some sticks to the fire.

Gabe's gut churned, his eyes widened, and he caught his breath as he turned toward Dove, "Which way?"

Dove scowled, pointed with her chin, "That way, the river and the stream from the mountains behind us merge. She said it was a good place for deer when the sun comes up."

Gabe glanced at the sky, dark with heavy clouds, but the sun struggled to give light for the day. He shook his head and went to the picketed horses and started saddling Ebony. Wolf paced at his side, anxiously waiting. Before he swung aboard, he slipped his rifle into the scabbard, checked his saddle bags, went to the shelter for a blanket and the coil of hemp rope, and secured them behind the cantle. He stepped aboard and swung the big stallion around just as Ezra walked into camp. "Cougar, went hunting down below, but . . ." he started, shaking his head.

"Yeah, I know!" declared Ezra, "Go on, I'll be right behind you!"

Gabe dug his heels into the big black, but Ebony was already stepping out, sensing the tense nature of his rider. The horse, man and wolf all had an uncanny connection as if each could read the mind of the other and Ebony stepped up to a canter as they followed the trail around the point of land that obscured the outlet of the lake. Another glance to the sky told of the fast-moving storm that was walking on spindly legs of lightning, thunder rolling along the high country to announce its approach. Low rolling hills stood between Gabe and the river channel, but Cougar's tracks followed the trail through the sparse trees between the long ridge and the rolling hills.

The strawberry roan ridden by Cougar showed tracks that told they had left at a canter, hooves digging toe first into the soft dirt of the trail. It was just a quarter mile from the point by the lake shore to the narrow valley that carried the run-off stream that meandered toward the confluence with the bigger river as it came from the lake. When they neared the edge of the trees, the crack of lightning startled both horse and rider as it split a tall dead snag of a tree that had stood as a sentinel atop the ridge. Fire flared but was quickly extinguished by the downpour and the storm marched on, spreading its ephemeral wings across the tall mountains and the rolling hills beside the lake. Wind stirred the waters into dancing whitecaps, moving in rhythm to the pounding drums of the thunder. Ezra pulled up beside Gabe and had to holler to be heard, "Spotted her yet?"

"No!" He pointed at the tracks in the trail, "But she came this way!"

The cloudburst pulled its plug, and the men and horses were drenched in an instant. The horses, a little skittish, rolled their skin a little, turning back to look at their riders, but received only a pet on the neck and some words to calm them. Both men had what some were calling oilskins, canvas duck coated with linseed oil and made into a type of coat, but they had been used for ground cover and were back at camp. They wore their wool union suits under their buckskins and the buckskins shed most of the water but were soon soaked through.

"So, what do you want to do?" shouted Ezra, looking at Gabe through the downpour.

Cougar had been watching the rapid approach of the storm but searched the narrow valley for any movement. She was anxious to get a deer, or even an elk, anything to provide fresh meat for them to wait out this storm and the following day to allow the trail to dry enough to travel. With four adults and four youngsters, their rations were quickly depleting and fresh meat after a long winter of smoked venison would be a treat as well as a necessity. She stepped down to look at the sign at the edge of the trail, fresh tracks from several deer. She stood, looking in the direction where the tracks left the trail, searching the willows and creek bank for deer.

She spotted movement, saw three doe, two fawn, and a button buck, tiptoeing to the water. She smiled, picking the buck or the doe without a fawn, and swung aboard the roan, intent on moving closer, using the trees for cover, before she took a shot with her bow. She had no sooner settled into the seat than the sudden cloudburst let loose and a torrent of rain smashed down as if she had ridden under a water-fall. The roan pranced nervously, head high and ears pricked, but Cougar held the reins tight, controlling the skittish gelding. She heard the crack of lightning and the instantaneous roll of thunder and gigged her mount from the trees. A roar came from the moun-tains and Cougar frowned, looking up the wide draw, but a blinding flash of lightning and the explosion as the bolt struck a towering ponderosa not a hundred feet away, startled the roan and Cougar.

The roan turned and took off at a run, following the trail that shadowed the stream in the valley bottom. With nose pointed into the wind, mane flying, and tail lifted like the flag on an ocean-going schooner, the horse flew through the trees, blindly following the narrow trail. Cougar held tight, pulling on the reins against the stubborn and frightened roan. She heard the increasing roar behind her, adding to her confu-sion and fear, but unknowing what was causing the sound, then sudden realization filled her heart with fear, making her glance over her shoulder. A wall of whitewater was chasing her down the narrow valley, riding the course of the run-off stream, carrying the water from the cloudburst that had drenched the

mountains and hills near the lake, even the overflow
from the lake had joined at the confluence and now
the massive wall roared like the monster of tales told
over fires that would gobble up everything in its path.
In less than a mile, the valley narrowed and the rimrock butte stood close beside the stream bed, a wide
talus slope pushing the trail nearer the water.

Another bolt of lightning split the sky and buried
itself atop the butte, blasting a tree free of its roots
to send it crashing down the talus slope, causing the
lichen covered slide rock to cascade down to add to
the debris. Both horse and rider saw the rockslide
beginning high up, but the horse had the temper of a
grizzly bear with a sore tooth, and did not stutter a
step, charging headlong into the danger, until another
bolt slammed into the trees beside the trail.

The horse slid to a stop, reared up, eyes wide,
pawing at the sky, trying to defend itself from the
shower of sparks and the flare of fire atop the remaining snag of the exploded tree. The heavy trunk, split
three ways, toppled down, smashing to the ground in
front of the terrified horse.

The roan reared high again, pawing at the air,
fighting the weight of the woman on its back, and
began backstepping away from the branches that
waved in the wind as if chasing the red roan. Another
part of the trunk had fallen behind the horse and the
roan stumbled, tripped, and fell backwards. Cougar

had grabbed a handful of mane, held tight to the reins and dug her heels into the ribs of her mount, but when the horse reared so high, standing almost erect and stumbled backwards, she kicked free of the stirrups and pushed away as the roan tumbled over backwards, with both horse and rider crashing through the brush, slamming into the water. The wall of water ripping at the gear and clothes, dragging them under, and pushing them down.

7 / SEARCH

Gabe squinted, lifted the brim of his soggy hat, looking into the deluge. He could not see the ears of his horse; the water came in such a torrent. The wind howled through the trees with such intensity it drowned out the roll of thunder. But as soon as it struck, it lessened and the howl of the wind was replaced by the rumble of the flash flood that came in a raging wall of water, pushing debris with its foaming head then trodding it under as it spread across the valley floor, charging to the canyon beyond. Gabe stood in his stirrups, saw the murky foam that crested the mass of debris, glanced at Ezra as his heart pounded in his chest. His eyes flared wide, fear danced across his face, as he shouted, "She's hurt!"

He reined the big black around and took off down the trail at a run, matching the flash flood stride for stride. The trail rode the flank of the rolling hills, moving in and out of the timber as it paralleled the river. The crashing water showed white as it cascaded over rocks and pushed at the flash flood debris that crowded the banks. Gabe let Ebony have his head, trusting the sure-footed stallion as he stood in his stirrups, searching the roaring waters for any sign of Cougar Woman. His heart banged in his chest, he fought for breath, the rain obscuring his vision, but it was lessening just enough for him to scan the flood waters as he rode. Ezra followed close behind, watching both the river and his friend, fearful of what they might find.

The big black slid to a stop, almost unseating his rider, and the big wolf bounded over the rocks that blocked the trail. Gabe stood in his stirrups, saw the remains of the trees, now almost buried in the rock slide, and twisted to search the narrow bank and the cascading waters. Ezra stopped behind him and jumped to the ground, going to the edge, his toes in the water as he looked both upstream and down for any sign of the woman. Nothing showed, until he looked almost at his feet. He bent down and picked up the broken bow of Cougar, shook his head and lifted it to Gabe.

"That don't mean nothin'!" he roared, "We gotta find her!" Gabe jumped to the ground and took to the rocks, picking a path over, then stepped down and took the reins of the black to encourage him over the slide. The stallion trusted his friend and carefully picked his steps as he moved from rock to rock, shifting his weight and moving carefully, Gabe stepping backwards, gently tugging on the reins. It was not unlike crossing a wide patch of slide rock in the mountains, something they had done before, but still dangerous. One misstep could result in a fall or a step between stones that could break a leg, but the gravel and dirt that fell after the bigger rocks had filled in much of the way and within moments, the big black stretched out and lunged forward to the trail. Gabe stood, patting his horse on the neck, and talking to him, and heard Ezra say, "Go 'head on, I'll catch up!"

Gabe swung aboard and started along the trail, but staying as close to the water as possible, always searching for any indication of his woman or her horse. He looked up as he heard a roar and recognized the sound of water pushing through a canyon and realized the river would soon be engulfed between steep walls that would prevent his seeing the entire river. He lifted his eyes to the heavens, felt the last of the rain pelting his face and cried out, "You can't have her! I won't let her go!"

He dropped the reins to ground tie Ebony and slipped down the bank to water's edge, Wolf at his heels, and stood to search the rapids and murky water, but nothing showed. He trotted along the edge of the water, called out, "Cougar! Cougar Woman!"

and trotted further, stopping to search both shores as much as he could see, climbed atop a big rock and looked again. The river bent away from the trail, butting against the steep limestone cliffs that marked the entry to the deep canyon, but the current pushed trees, brush, and driftwood, into a pile at the point of the bend. Gabe frowned, shaded his eyes from the thin mist of rain and the shaft of sunlight that pushed through the clouds. Something was caught in the debris, but he could not make it out.

He slipped from the big rock, waded through the edge of the water, and stepped on the narrow sloping bank, grabbed a long branch of the tall ponderosa that dipped into the water, and moved around the abutment. As he neared the washed-up debris, the lowering flood waters receding, he saw what he thought was an animal, maybe a deer or elk, but he had to look closer. As he stepped on the uncertain footing of the pile of driftwood and branches, he neared the hair covered flank, then froze as he recognized the muddied coloring of the strawberry roan, Cougar's horse!

Ezra hollered down from the trail as he peered through the trees, "Find anything?"

"Her horse! But I've got to look more, too much debris!" shouted Gabe as he started digging through the debris, tossing branches, pulling at the trunks of bigger trees, twisting and jerking, trying to free the carcass of the horse from the pile of rubble. He tugged on one big branch, but the voice of Ezra just behind him gave him pause.

"I'll get up top and push with my legs. You pull from here," he instructed as he mounted the pile of logs. Within moments the last obstruction was freed, and they saw the carcass of the roan, neck broken, a leg broken, deep gashes on his belly, and only the headstall of the bridle remained. Gabe dug around in the debris until he was satisfied Cougar was not there, then stepped back and stared at the maw of the canyon and the low roar of cascading waters that dared him enter.

"I've got to find her!" he stated as he struggled free of the pile and started through the trees back to the trail. Ezra had brought Ebony along and both horses lifted their heads as the men returned. They mounted up and took to the trail, but Gabe soon reined up, looked through the trees to see the edge of the canyon further away, then took the coil of hemp rope, grabbed his brass telescope in its case, undid the blanket roll, and threw the blanket over his shoulder. He looked at Ezra, "You take Ebony with you, follow the trail, whenever it's clear for you to see, wait for me. If I find her and need your help, I'll fire a shot!" Ezra nodded, accepted Ebony's reins, and watched as Gabe and Wolf took to the trees, going to the canyon's rim to search for Cougar. Ezra took a deep breath and looked to the trail, nudged his bay onward and walked the horses through the trees.

What had been a frantic, almost panic, scampering to find Cougar, now became a quiet determination. Gabe scanned everything, in, near, or above the water. He knew Cougar was a good swimmer and a strong woman and he was confident that if anyone could survive this, she could and would. When the edge of the canyon walls prevented him from descending, he bellied down at the edge and searched everything in the canyon bottom. He had been in canyons just like this and knew there were innumerable places that could become havens, some that could not be seen from above, but he searched anyway, using his scope to probe every nook and cranny of the gorge.

Seeing nothing of interest, he stood and moved further downstream, saw a place where he could go to the bottom and quickly descended the steep slope, dropping to the narrow bank at water's edge. He looked everywhere, saw nothing, and climbed back to the top, muttering a prayer with each step, "Lord, please."

When Cougar splashed back into the water, she was quickly dragged under, the current grabbing at her with so many icy fingers, and she fought, kicking, and pulling herself to the surface. She sucked air, but the crashing waves drove her down again. She kicked, and reached out to grab at the water, pulling herself along with the current, knowing it was useless to fight against the savage storm waters. She tried to look for her roan, but the muddy waters had clouded her vision and she fought for air each time her head rose above the thrashing debris laden water.

She slapped at her head, pushing her hair away from her eyes, and saw a tree rolling and turning in the current. She kicked at the water and struggled to catch a branch, snagged it, and pulled, but the tree rolled, pushing the branch under and almost taking her with it, so she kicked back away, and tried to see another, bigger tree or log, anything. She was rapidly tiring, the current fighting against her every effort, the water robbing her of any warmth, and her muscles aching.

The crashing waters slammed her against a wall of rock as the river bent away from the cliff face, and she grabbed at her head, brought her hand back that showed blood, and fought against the current to push away from the cliff, but it fought her, pinning her against the rock face, until she rolled over and over, the current fighting, until she dove into the water, and kicked away. The sudden rush of the current grabbed at her and carried her under, tumbling her end over end, disorienting her until she did not know how to find air. She kicked and pulled, letting the driving current carry her, swimming with it as she felt her lungs would burst, then broke from the water, sucking in air and letting the current move her along. She looked about, saw nothing but steep canyon walls, and fear rose ever higher, her heart pounding in her chest, as she fought to breathe. She twisted around, and around, looking for anything to grab onto and saw another tree, a big, uprooted spruce that seemed to ride the waves, branches outstretched, and inviting. She pushed for the tree, grabbed a branch, and pulled herself near. She tried to climb on, but once she lifted her upper torso onto the trunk, she grabbed a far branch, and hung on, resting, looking for any way out, but seeing none.

The current was still pushing hard, the walls of the canyon slipping quickly by, but she noticed the river was twisting around, bending back on itself, crashing against the canyon walls. Most river canyons held few twists and turns, usually carving its way in direct paths, but this one Cougar recognized as the canyon that sided the trail to her people's country. Just the thought that the river would pass the camp of her people somehow encouraged Cougar, even though she knew it would be the equivalent of many days ride before reaching the land of the Shoshone.

8 / RECOVERY

The current was relentless, pushing, driving, tearing at Cougar Woman as if she had broken the rules of nature by surviving and clinging to the tree. Most of the branches had been torn off and as the waves crashed against the sheer cliffs of the canyon, she was able to see but what she saw was disheartening. No escape was offered, any break in the walls was quickly swept past as the thrashing of the current drove her on, yet she clung to the rough barked tree with all her strength. She looked past the white caps of the rapids that smashed against a big boulder in mid-stream, saw the sharp bend in the river made malevolent by the slick face of the limestone wall. The current churned, crashing against the unyielding cliff face and twisting everything it carried in every direction possible. The roar of the rapids magnified by the narrow confines.

Driven against the cliff, the tree turned, twisted,

and splintered its length, the few remaining branches driven under and Cougar Woman with them. She kicked, grabbed, fought and pulled, reaching out for anything, but the force of the water held her against the cliff, forcing any air from her lungs, when a broken log smashed into the side of her head, knocking her against the wall, and blackness enveloped her.

Gabe followed the river into the canyon, staying atop the cliffs to search the water below. Time and again his hopes were raised, then dashed again, as he searched the washed-up piles of debris, hoping for any sighting of Cougar. The river twisted and turned, each cut back catching logs, brush, trees, and the bodies of small animals that had been caught in the flood. Ezra waited just past a wide bend; the trail pushed close to the canyon wall by a rising butte. He saw Gabe walking toward him, his demeanor telling of his failure.

"Nothin'!" he grumbled, dropping to a grass covered hump.

"Looks like the water's gone down, mebbe we'll do better," offered Ezra, searching for anything that would pick up Gabe's spirits a mite. They were on a shoulder that was held in place by a line of rimrock at the canyon's lip, scattered sage and greasewood, some bunch grass covered the sloping shoulder. From Gabe's seat he could see into the canyon, but his discouragement dulled his vision.

"Lemme have your scope, I wanna look around that bend yonder," stated Ezra, motioning to the sharp bend of the river that twisted past the point of a finger ridge pushing into the canyon.

Gabe held it out to his friend, and lay back in the grass, exhausted and losing hope. Ezra walked out to the edge of the rimrock, went to one knee and lifted the scope. He scanned the rugged face of the many fingered talus slope that dropped into the river, pushing the stream past and bending it around the point of the ridge. The steep sided talus offered nothing for a landing or catch all for debris, the cascades rushing past. Ezra stood, frowning, and walked further along the rimrock until he could see past the sharp bend. He was surprised to see the canyon opened up to show a stretch of wide flat where the river split into several rivulets, each one weaving its way down and around the scattered debris that had been caught on the brush and snags of the many islands that formed when the river split.

There were logs, snags, brush piled at the point of each island, with greater piles of debris at the far edge where the current waned and shallow water eddied past. Ezra stretched out the scope, sat down with legs hanging over the rimrock, and slowly scanned as much of the mouth of the flat land valley as he could see, sighting the carcass of a spotted fawn, a coyote, a cow elk, and many piles of driftwood and other debris. One pile showed the weathered grey of old logs and driftwood that had held its place even with the flash flood that splattered its mark on the canyon walls and the washed-up gravel of the islands. He looked at the pile, but something was different. It wasn't a bark covered tree, or the carcass of an animal, but a splash of black and brown suggested something else.

"Gabe! Gabe! Come look!" he hollered, keeping his eye on the spot of interest.

Gabe came to his side, shielding his eyes to look where Ezra pointed and felt the scope against his chest as Ezra said, "There, in the mouth of that wide draw where the driftwood is scattered on the far side!" pointing before them.

Gabe dropped to one knee, rested his elbow on the other and stretched out the brass telescope. He adjusted the focus, held it steady, and said, "Maybe, maybe." He dropped the scope and looked at Ezra and the canyon walls, "But how am I gonna get down there?"

Ezra stood and looked along the edge of the canyon, pointed to the talus slopes, "There! That last outcropping of rock beside the talus! I can lower you on your rope, but you'll have to find your own way for the last bit!"

Gabe jumped to his feet and started at a run to

the shoulder with the talus, Wolf at his side. Ezra retrieved the horses, stepped aboard his bay and leading Ebony, followed close behind his friend. Gabe ran around the sharp bend and onto the shoulder that overlooked the narrow valley below. He glanced back at Ezra as he lifted the rope that hung over his neck and shoulder, dropped it to the ground and carefully stepped closer to the edge. He leaned out, peering over the edge, and looking at the route that was chosen from their previous promontory. It was a narrow chute that lay below a long stretch of rock that dropped at a steep angle into the river bottom. As Ezra reined up beside him, and dropped to the ground, he pointed, "If you tie it off to your pommel, and let your horse take the strain, I'll back down as far as I can, hopefully to the beginning of that chute, and from there on it looks like I slide!"

Wasting little effort and time, the rope was quickly secured as Gabe rolled the blanket and draped it over one shoulder, tying it close to his belt. He looked at Wolf who stood looking back and forth, obviously upset, then to Ezra, "Alright, here goes!" and backed to the edge and slowly stepped off. He heard Wolf whimper, growl, and saw him drop down to stretch out his front feet and put his head between them as he watched Gabe lower himself. He overhanded it down the shear drop until his feet touched down, then he paused, catching his breath, and looking over his shoulder to the targeted chute. He backhanded it further down, cautiously picking each step where able, and as he reached the end of the rope, he was at the peak of the chute. He took a deep breath, turned around for a better look, saw several dead trees across the chute, probably from an ancient blowdown, and tried to mentally mark his path. With a glance over his shoulder, he sat down, legs outstretched and let go the rope.

He started sliding, bouncing off some rocks, kicking at others as he dug his heels in to slow his descent. He looked up to see a big grey log lying across the chute and stretched out flat to slide under. His feet hit some loose shale and rocks, but he plowed his way through, the steep descent drawing him onward until his feet hit the water. His sudden stop surprised him as he saw the shallow and clear water at his feet. Obviously, the storm waters had passed, and he waded across the shallow, looking toward the debris pile on the far side. With no bank on the closer edge, he waded through the water until the valley opened and he climbed the grassy shore at the edge of the debris pile. He stood, leaning over to see the opposite end of the pile and caught his breath. The splash of black was her hair and the brown, her waterlogged buckskins, ripped and torn, but mostly still there. He scrambled over the grey logs, quickly reaching her side, and stretched out his hand to tenderly touch her. He saw the rise and fall of her back and gently rolled her over. Her face and arms were scratched, some wounds bleeding slightly, a big gouge above her right ear showed blood, but she was breathing. Her forehead wrinkled as the bright sun shone warm on her face, but her eyes did not open. Her breathing was ragged, and as he moved her, a moan escaped her lips.

He lifted her, balancing himself on a big grey log, and carefully stepped down from the pile. He waded through the water to pass the pile, then stepped onto the grassy bank to lay her gently in the thick green grass. He looked at each wound carefully, noting the worst one at the side of her head, and another on her left knee. He stretched out the blanket to cover her and looked around for something to use as a poultice or bandage, saw some tall skinny flowers just starting to show yellow and he whispered, "Wound Wort!" He came to his feet and went to collect several of the long skinny leaves and the few buds that had opened to show the beginning of the bright yellow bloom.

He came back to the side of Cougar, gave her a quick check, and fetched a couple of rocks from the riverbank to grind the leaves and buds of the goldenrod into a poultice. With a torn off corner of the blanket, he washed her wounds, applied the poultice, and bound them with strips of the blanket. She seemed to breathing more evenly but had not opened her eyes. Gabe sat back on his haunches and was startled to hear water splashing and turned to see Ezra aboard his big bay, leading Ebony, as Wolf came from the water, shook his rolling hide to shed the water, and ran to the side of his friend. He sniffed at Cougar, and started licking her face as Gabe said, "Easy boy, easy. She's hurtin'!" and pushed at the wolf's shoulder to move him away, but the wolf frowned as he looked at Gabe then back at Cougar to see her eyelids twitch, as she struggled to bring her hand over her eyes. The shadow of Wolf covered her face, but she was blinded by the brightness of the sunlight. With a moan, she struggled, "Where . . .?"

Gabe leaned close, "You're with us. You're gonna be fine!"

"What . . .?"

"You were caught in a flash flood and went for a swim," explained Gabe, smiling broadly, relief showing on his face.

"Ummm, my head," she mumbled, reaching to touch the bandage. She frowned, struggling to open her eyes wider and look at Gabe, but the black wolf licked at her face, making her pull away, "Wolf!" but reached up to touch the thick scruff, and pull him closer.

Wolf wagged his tail and smacked Gabe with it, making the man push him away, "Hey! Back off! It's my turn!" complained Gabe, leaning in closer to Cougar. His face just inches from hers, he spoke softly, "You had me scared, but the good Lord answered our prayers."

Cougar forced a smile and put her arms around Gabe's neck and pulled him close.

9 / RECOUP

Cougar rolled from her blankets, looked around at the empty shelter and pushed back the flap to see the others gathered near the fire. She crawled from the lean-to and slowly stood, feeling the soreness and stabbing pain shoot down her legs and pound against the side of her head. She staggered to the side, caught herself on the lean-to rope, and stood still, breathing deep and looking around slowly. She stretched and twisted her torso and noticed everyone watching her as Bobcat came running her direction, arms wide, "Momma!" he shouted as he crashed into her, almost knocking her down.

She laughed as she bent down to hold the little boy close to her legs as he wrapped his arms around her, laying his cheek against her leg. She looked up, saw Gabe coming near holding Fox in his arms who had his one arm outstretched toward her. She smiled as she stood erect and reached for the little one. She looked at Gabe, "How long have I been sleeping?"

"Not long, day and a half or so," he chuckled as he pulled Bobcat away from his mother's legs and nudged him back to the others. He put his arm around her waist to steady her, took Fox from her and swung him to his back, and started back to the fire.

Cougar looked at the sky, surprised to see dusk coming on, and shook her head as she found a seat on the grey log beside the fire. Strips of fresh venison hung suspended over the fire, broiling and dripping juices into the flames. Sliced turnips, cattail shoots, and potatoes sizzled in the pan, and coffee steamed at the side. She lifted her eyebrows as she looked, "Ummm, smells good! I am hungry!"

Gabe chuckled, "You haven't eaten for almost three days, so, yeah, reckon you are!"

She nodded to the meat, "Is that the meat I was looking for?"

"Prob'ly. When we were bringin' you back from your swim, that little buck stepped out in front of us and said, 'I'm the one she wanted!', so, there he hangs!" explained Gabe, nodding to the carcass hanging from a limb of the ponderosa.

Ezra was reaching for the coffee pot when Wolf came to his feet, growling and looking through the trees toward the trail by lakeside. Ezra looked at Gabe, and the men snatched up their rifles and disappeared into the trees. The women gathered the children close, but watched the trail and Wolf as he stood, head lifted, orange eyes flaring and lip snarling. Cougar put her hand on his scruff, "Easy boy, easy. Let's see who they are," as she looked to the trees and the trail below to see several riders, natives, turn toward their camp.

Cougar stood, Wolf at her side, his side against her leg, and watched three riders come through the trees. Others stayed at the trail, watching. When the men broke from the trees, they reined up, side by side, glaring at the women and children by the fire. The shadows of dusk masked their faces, but Cougar saw they wore no war paint, but that did not mean they were friendly. One man gigged his horse forward a step, sat erect, moving his shoulders back and head high, and spoke in Shoshone, "Who are you and why are you here?" he growled.

Cougar thought she recognized the man when he moved from the shadows, but she was back from the fire and in a shadow herself. Wolf stayed close as Cougar stepped forward, still in the shadows, "Who does Snake Eater think he is that he could question me?"

The man snapped back as if he had been hit, then leaned forward, squinting. "You speak our tongue, but I do not know you!"

"I am the warrior who spared your life! I was your war leader when you followed Little Mountain!" explained Cougar, enjoying the frustration showing on

Snake Eater's face. Little Mountain had been the man who sought to destroy Cougar Woman and take her place as the war leader of the Tukkutikka Shoshone but was defeated by Cougar, and ultimately killed when he sought vengeance and attacked Gabe and company, only to be taken down and killed by Wolf. Snake Eater had been a close friend to Little Mountain but knew the big man had been wrong when he sought vengeance. Snake Eater had returned to his people and his family, having learned a valuable lesson about people.

Snake Eater slipped to the ground, walked slowly toward the woman and when she stepped from the shadows, a broad smile painted his face, and he came forward quickly to greet his former war leader. The two clasped forearms, slapping their shoulders with their free hands, and laughing. "Doya dukubichi', it is good to see you!" he declared, looking down at Wolf who had not moved away from Cougar. He lifted his eyes to the edge of the camp to see the men come from the trees, rifles held across their chests.

"Spirit Bear, Black Buffalo, good to see you!"

Cougar turned toward her man, "It is Snake Eater," declared Cougar.

The name brought many memories from years past, but Gabe and Ezra came forward to see the man and his band. Snake Eater motioned to his men, one turning away to tell the others, and soon the clearing was filled with the warriors of the Shoshone hunting party. Dove and Cougar put more steaks on the fire, and Dove pushed several camas roots into the coals. As they visited, Snake Eater told them they were less than two days from the encampment of the Tukkutikka who made their summer camp near the Snake River east of the big lake where the Snake flowed from the big waters. It was good news to the travelers, knowing they would soon be among Cougar's people and would spend a few days visiting.

The hunting party spent the night with the travelers but departed at first light to resume their hunt. They were intent on finding a herd of elk to replenish the stores for their village. Gabe and company resumed their travel, Cougar still somewhat sore from the tumbling in the flood waters, but her wounds were healing well and the many bruises fading. They made the first day a leisurely one, and Ezra bagged a moose that would provide both meat for them, and a welcome gift for Cougar's family.

Cougar rode the spotted rump appaloosa, who showed her friskiness at such a long time without being ridden, but Cougar mastered her and kept her well in check and the two soon became close friends. Cougar's ways of kindness and firmness won her over and Cougar looked at Gabe, "Why didn't I start riding her sooner? She's got a smooth gait and she's smart! I really like her!"

"So, you're saying she's now your horse?"

"Ummhmmm, and I believe your son has eyes for that yearling," nodding toward the colt at the spotted mare's side. The colt was marked much like his mother and had soft eyes, and a muscular chest and rump. The long back and strong legs showed the colt would develop into a fine animal.

Gabe grinned, glanced at Bobcat and the colt, and said, "It wouldn't hurt for the two of them to get better acquainted. Maybe I'll work with 'em, let him sit on the colt, talk to him and such, and they'll probably become good friends and grow up together."

Cougar nodded, smiling, "Then you'll have to let Ebony breed her," pointing to the spotted mare, "again to get a colt for Fox!"

"Sounds reasonable," answered Gabe.

It was mid-afternoon as they rode into the village of the Tukkutikka band of the Shoshone people and many immediately recognized their former war leader. Several came to Cougar's side as they led the horses into the village, greeting her and the others. Youngsters shied away from the big wolf, hiding behind their mothers but peeking around to look at the strange sight of a wolf walking with people. When they neared the central compound of the village, Little Weasel and his woman stood before their lodge, stoic expressions on their faces as they stood, arms across their chests, waiting for the visitors to come forward.

Gabe and Cougar Woman stood side by side as they greeted Little Weasel, the leader of the village. When Little Weasel recognized Cougar Woman, his countenance changed and he stepped forward to greet her and Gabe, - Spirit Bear. "It is good for you to return to your people." He frowned when he saw the wound, although it was healing, on the side of her head and he looked to Spirit Bear, "Does she not obey you?"

Gabe tried his best to show a stern look, but failing, he explained, "She has been a good wife, but a poor swimmer. She had to learn that flood waters are not good for bathing or swimming."

Little Weasel quickly read the facial expressions of the man before him and let a slow grin cross his face, "I see." He glanced at Cougar Woman, "It was hard to teach her as a war leader also. Stubborn," he added, shaking his head with a serious expression.

Cougar looked from Gabe to Little Weasel, frowning and mumbled, "Men!" but before she could say more, she saw Two Horses and Pretty Cloud coming quickly toward them. She smiled and turned to greet her father and mother, embracing both and quickly turning to bring the boys forward to meet their grandparents. Little Weasel looked at Gabe, frowned, and said, "She does not pay attention to us," shaking his head, but grinning broadly. He looked at Gabe,

"We will talk again. Go now, visit with family."

"Thank you, Little Weasel. We will talk again," answered Gabe as he turned to speak to Cougar's parents. They were welcomed and directed to make their camp near the lodge of Cougar's family, and Dove went with Cougar while the men tended the horses and packs. They looked forward to a few days with her people and the time to rest the animals and themselves.

10 / DESERT

"They have been following us for three days now!" declared Diego, looking at Capitan Almeida. "What are they waiting for? What do they want?" he pleaded.

Francisco de Almeida could not answer the questions of his lieutenant and he was just as fearful as the others, but he could not let it show. He glanced at the line of mounted Indians that rode the crest of the hills to the north, and answered, "Eh! Who knows? They are savages and have probably never seen such as us. They are curious is all!" But he knew it would be more than curiosity that would make anyone follow this band of explorer through the hot desert land they now traversed. He had used his telescope when they first saw the small band of natives shadowing them and could tell they had only bows and lances for weapons. They were a dark people, most wearing a cloth headband, breechcloths, and high-topped moccasins. They did nothing to shade themselves from the harsh and blinding sun and the terrain offered little refuge. With scattered piñon, cedar, and juniper, none more than ten feet tall, there was no shade. The land bore only cactus and tufts of buffalo grass, with very little water.

Although they had traded for more horses from the Pima and all the men were now mounted, the extra animals required more water. This morning they left the headwaters of the small east fork of the Gila, hoping to reach the Rio Bravo del Norte, or what some called the Rio Grande, but their maps were old and inaccurate. They were traveling due west and with the sun at its highest point, sweat dripped from the men, lather foamed on the horses and mules, and there was no breeze. The men carried canteens, but it was scarcely enough water for the men, leaving nothing for the animals.

The Capitan looked at the natives that rode the ridges, noting there were now seven. He spoke softly to his lieutenant, Diego, "There are seven," nodding toward the riders.

"There were only four. Does that mean we are nearing their village that there are more?" he asked, fearful of the answer.

"How should I know? I think we need to stop this! I am tired of them following and watching!" declared the Capitan.

"What should we do?" asked Diego.

"There," suggested Francisco, pointing with his chin to the wide draw before them. "They will ride the ridge and are within rifle range. They do not have rifles and maybe do not know about them. Pick your best marksmen, bring them up alongside. When we reach that draw, they will drop down, use their saddles as a rest, and shoot them," nodding toward the ridge riders, "from their horses!"

Diego frowned as he looked at his Capitan, then nodded and pulled his mount to the side to wait for the others. As they rode past, he chose two of the sergeants, Duarte Fernandes, and Antonio De Noli, and six of the men. As they were chosen, Diego instructed, "Ride forward with your rifles ready. One line beside the others, Sergeant Fernandes will be in the lead."

As Diego rode beside the column and passed each shooter, he explained, "At the order, drop to the right side of your mount, use your saddle for a rest, and pick your target, but wait for the order, then shoot!" Each man acknowledged the order with a nod or an answer, as they had become accustomed to the necessity for strict obedience to the commands given. Many of these men had fought in the War of the First Coalition and the War of the Pyrenees, some had been blooded, but left the military for this expedition, not expecting to fight.

The Capitan watched the riders, glanced at his men

who were watching him for the order, and as they neared his chosen point of the wide draw, a glance showed the riders had sky lined themselves at no more than fifty yards. The Capitan turned toward the men, giving the order, "Dismount!" just loud enough for the men to hear. They quickly reined up and swung down, laying their M1752 muskets across the seats of their saddles and bringing them to full cock. Each man picking his target and within seconds, heard the order, "FIRE!" The conglomerate of blasts sounded like the roar of a cannon. Smoke spat from the smooth bore muskets and hung like a grey cloud before them. The men quickly began reloading, using the paper cartridges to pour gunpowder down the barrel, jam the casing of the cartridge after the powder as wadding, then the .69 caliber ball. The ramrod pushed it all down to be firmly seated. The shooter put powder in the pan, slapped the frizzen down, and brought the hammer to full cock as he lifted the rifle for another shot. The cloud of smoke had dissipated, but there were no remaining targets.

The first blast had struck four of the riders, driving them from their horses to the ground. Two others remained seated, but with handfuls of mane and gripping the rein tightly, they rode off the ridge to disappear into the valleys beyond. One man was not hit and led the flight of the others. Each of the shooters looked to their Capitan as he barked, "Good shooting!

Mount up but keep your rifles ready!"

Diego was at the Capitan's side as he sounded the order, "At a canter, Ho!" and kicked his horse to a canter. He looked at Diego, "We need to put some distance behind us in case their village is close!"

"Without water, we cannot keep this pace long!" answered Diego, looking at the lather on his horse's neck.

The Capitan leaned forward, pointed to a ravine, "There!" and pointed his horse toward the narrow declivity. They rode into the close sided ravine that sloped downhill, reining up as a bend offered some semblance of shade from the stifling heat.

Diego ordered the men, "Tend to the animals first! Give them water from your canteens, then rub them down. There's bunch grass there," nodding to the upper end of the ravine, "Keep your rifles at the ready!"

Pisago Cabezón glared at the man before him, "If it is as you say, these men are not of the desert!"

"It is as I say, my chief. It was like the thunder of a great storm and a cloud covered them! This many," holding up four fingers, "of our men fell, blood all over. Two others were wounded but fell behind and I do not know if they live. I alone was unhurt. Perhaps the gods allowed me to live to tell our people of this great danger!" The man known as Ponce stood with head down, shaking it side to side, glancing up at the chief of the *Tsoka-ne-nde* band of the Chiricahua. The chief remembered tales of the grandfathers that told of a people that wore metal hats and covered their chest with metal, he had even seen these things, but that was long ago. He had also heard of these weapons of thunder, but his people had never encountered them.

"I will speak with our elders," stated the chief and turned away, dismissing the man.

The war chief known as Tapilá, stepped from the brush wickiup, saw a waiting warrior, and motioned him close. "Go, gather two hands of warriors. We go against the killers of our men."

Tapilá swung aboard his mount, waved to his men to follow and the band of more than a dozen proven warriors of the Chiricahua rode from the village. The war chief glanced at the sun as it stood above the jagged western horizon and waved Ponce to his side. The chief glared at the man, "We will go to where our men fell, from there we will follow the intruders and take them at night!"

Ponce looked at his chief, frowning, and with a slight shake of his head, he answered, "We have never attacked an enemy at night!"

Tapilá scowled, "We will this night. We cannot go against these thunder weapons when they can see us. These are the words of the council!"

At the statement that these words came from the

council, Ponce knew he could not argue. Although his people believed that no one can speak for another and that any warrior had the right to choose what he was to do, it was different when the council of elders spoke for they thought only of the people of their village and each one must do their part to protect the village.

Tapilá motioned for Ponce to take the lead and go to the place where they were attacked. It would be required for them to return the bodies to the village for the families to properly tend to them. The bodies would be dressed and buried with the deceased most treasured possessions. The family's home and the man's other possessions would be burned, and the family would move away to avoid the dead man's ghost.

"I do not think we will see any more of the natives, but you will post a guard," ordered Capitan de Almeida, speaking to Diego Garcia, the lieutenant. "We will leave before first light. There will be ample moonlight and the sky is clear. Travel will be easier in the early morning. Have the men clean their weapons and turn in early."

"Si, mi Capitan. Will we reach the Rio Bravo del Norte soon?"

"I do not know, but perhaps one or two days will tell. We should be close," answered the Capitan. He had referenced the maps entrusted to him by his uncle, the Brigadier Bustamante y Guerra, copies of maps made in 1776 by the Domínguez-Escalante expedition. He had been instructed to follow the Rio Grande north until it turned west, then cross a long valley that had a long ridge of mountains on the east side, then over the mountains to another river called the Arkansa. With a month of travel behind them, they faced at least another month before reaching the river.

Bustamante had studied the previous expeditions that entered this land beginning with the Narváez expedition of 1527 and the Coronado expedition of 1540. The legend of the Seven Cities of Gold was the motivation behind the Coronado expedition, and most believed that Quivira lay in the plains far to the east of the mountains. But the study by Bustamante had convinced him and others that the cities of Gold were near the headwaters of the river called Arkansa in the high mountains and had financed and put together this expedition to find them.

The band of explorers turned in at dusk, relieved at the cooler night air, and were quickly sound asleep, all but the posted guards. Diego reported to the Capitan, "The men have turned in and the guards chosen. There is a guard at each end of the camp, and each will be relieved in two hours."

"Good! Now get some sleep yourself. Tomorrow

will be a long day!"

Diego nodded and went to his blankets, already laid out under the branches of a bushy juniper. He was away from the others, choosing to be alone and dependent only on himself. Within moments, his snoring and grunts joined the chorus of the others.

11 / CLASH

Diego was restless. The shooting of the natives was unprovoked, and their Capitan seemed unconcerned about any consequences. Although his own experience with natives such as these was limited to those incurred since they left the ships, he believed that anyone was deserving of fair consideration and treatment. He rolled from his blankets, and walked to check on the picketed animals, just something to do to keep his mind from running rampant. It was quiet in the camp, several of the men were snoring or grumbling in their sleep, but the sounds of nightbirds and cicadas could still be heard. He stood at the head of his mount, a black gelding that came from Spain and Diego had claimed while they were still aboard ship. He spoke softly to the horse, stroking his head and neck, until the gelding lifted his head, ears pricked as he looked past Diego.

Diego turned and scanned the camp, watching for any movement in the dim moonlight. He heard a bit of a scuffle from the far end of the camp where he had stationed the guard, then quiet. He did not move, staying in the shadows beside his black, yet watching the tree line and hillside for any movement. He slipped his pistol from his belt, held it close and with his free hand over the hammer to stifle any sound, brought the pistol to full cock. He glanced at his horse who stood still, shoulder muscles twitching and ears forward watching the darkness, and looked in the direction of the second guard, closer to the horses.

A flash in the moonlight betrayed the attacker and Diego fired, unsure of his shot but knowing the blast would alarm the camp. The pistol bucked and emitted lead and smoke, as Diego heard a grunt, followed by the scrambling and shouting of the awakened men. Another pistol roared as screams from the attackers split the darkness. More pistols barked, then the deeper throated roar of rifles spoke into the night. Every man had been equipped with a pistol and rifle and ordered to always keep their weapons near. Diego shouted, "Pick your shots!" warning the men so they would not shoot each other.

The continual roar of pistols and rifles had startled the Chiricahua for they believed the men could not use the weapons in the dark. At the scream of Tapilá, the warriors broke off the battle, and fled.

When the war cries stopped, the men of the camp stood, looking at one another and into the dim moon light, but it appeared the attackers had fled. "Reload!" ordered Diego as he walked into the midst of the men. "Anyone hurt?" he asked, looking from one to another. There was grumbling and mumbling, but no one spoke of wounds until one of the men said, "I think the guards were killed."

Diego went to the nearest guard post to find Nuno da Cunha lying on his face, blood covering most of his back where he had been knifed from behind. Diego rolled him over, saw sightless eyes staring into the dark. He stood and ordered, "Sergeant Corte-Real, get two men and bury this man!" Diego walked the length of the camp, passing a confused Capitan as he did, and came to the side of the first guard who lay contorted on his back, his legs askew and his throat slit. He remembered this man's name as Pêro Dias. He stood and shouted to the others, "Sergeant Fernandes, you, two men, bury this man!"

As he left the side of the guard, another of their men came to him, "Lieutenant Garcia, my friend, Pedro Teixeira, is dead. His head was split by an attacker, but I killed him."

Garcia frowned, "Where was he?" for he had not seen any of his men that had been injured when he walked through the camp.

"We had gone to the trees for, you know," cocking his head to the side, motioning to the trees, "and he was struck by a hatchet. But I shot the man with my pistol."

"Good, good. Get Sergeant De Noli to have a detail bury Pedro."

"Si, si," he replied, turning away from Garcia.

The lieutenant went to the side of Capitan Almeida and spoke, "We lost three men. I believe we killed at least that many attackers, but they took the bodies with them. I suggest we leave as soon as possible, before they return with more warriors."

The Capitan had been staring into the darkness, his eyes glassy, but he turned to face the Lieutenant, "Uh, si, si, we should leave right away. Tell the men."

Garcia frowned, looking at the Capitan who appeared to be dazed, but realized the man had never seen battle like so many of the men, Garcia included. While others were fighting wars, this man had been home in his posh estate, playing the part of a member of the wealthy ruling class that never bloodied their hands with such things. Garcia shook his head as he walked away, speaking to the men as he strode among them, assigning duties to each one so the expedition could once again be under way.

One more day brought them to the banks of the Rio Grande. The men were joyous at the sight of water and rode their horses directly into the rippling eddy at water's edge. The animals drank deeply, and the men slipped into the water, splashing, and laughing. The long hot days of dusty travel through the foothills and prairie had sapped their strength and energy, but the cool waters of the wide river were just what they needed.

Diego frowned as he looked at the Capitan, who stood on the banks, shading his eyes and looking to the far side as if searching for something. He approached quietly and asked, "Is there something you look for, Capitan?"

Almeida turned quickly toward Diego, scowling, then nodded, "Si, si. There was a pueblo here and a mission, but I believe that mound," pointing across the river, "is all that remains." He paused as he looked again, then turned back to Diego, "This trail," nodding to the wide well-used trail that paralleled the river, "is known as the *Camino Real de Tierra Adentro.* It has been the trade route between Mexico City and the north for two centuries. We will travel north on this trail." He stepped away from the bank, reached for the reins on his mount to pull him back from the water, and added, "We will take a day to rest and repair our gear," ordered Capitan Almeida, scowling at Lieutenant Garcia. "You should get control of those men. What if we were attacked while they play in the water?!"

"I will stand guard for them, mi Capitan. The

men need this, and it would do us good as well. A bath would feel good to get rid of this dust," he declared, slapping at his doublet, raising a cloud of dust between them.

The Capitan snorted and turned away, grumbling as he led his horse to the water, upstream from the others. He dipped water in his cupped palm and drank, glancing at the men below him, shaking his head all the while and thinking of the grand estate he left behind in Spain. But his family had exhausted their inheritance and were living hand to mouth, which had prompted him to accept the offer of his brother-in-law to make this expedition. If it were as successful as he hoped, their fortunes would be restored and maybe even increased. Then he would become what he was meant to be, a part of the gentry of the city and nation. He grinned at the thought and stood, glaring downstream at the rabble he commanded. He lifted one eyebrow, curled his lip, and showed his disdain for those that were less than his nobility.

Four days of following the Camino Real trail north had become repetitious and tiring. The terrain varied little, greenery near the river, dry rolling hills away from the water. Piñon, cedar, and juniper trees, a myriad of cactus from the tall barrel cactus and the scrawny cholla to the sprawling clusters of prickly pear and hedge-hog cactus, the only variety being the blossoms of bright yellow, orange, red and pink. The diet of the men varied from rabbit to deer to javalina, although some tried armadillo and quickly discarded it in favor of venison.

They rode the west bank of the river, the flat lands riding high above the wide river bottom. Late on the fourth day, Diego, who had been scouting ahead, came back to the column at a trot and reined up before the Capitan. After a quick salute, he began, "Finally! Some sign of civilization! A mission, Capitan! There are natives working in the courtyard and a friar watching over them. I did not go close enough to talk; I knew you would be anxious to hear." He reined around to side the Capitan who had not slowed as Diego gave his report.

"It is good. According to what the map tells us, that should be the *San Agustín de la Isleta Mission*. That would mean *La Villa de Alburquerque* is about a half day further. We will resupply there," stated the Capitan.

Diego grinned, then asked, "Will we push on this day to get to the village, or do we camp beside the river and the mission?"

"How far to the mission?" asked the Capitan.

"Not far! Maybe an hour, less," resolved Diego, hoping to continue to the village.

"We will decide when we reach the mission," declared the Capitan, as he gigged his mount to a trot, and then to a canter.

Diego watched Capitan Almeida move away, then turned to signal the men, "At a canter, now!" The dust rolled high behind them, most of the column caught within the brown cloud, but the quick step was a mood breaker for the men, each leaning into the canter, smiling broadly as dust painted their teeth, prompting the men to lift scarves over their faces, but keeping up the pace.

Diego saw the tall bastions of the mission and motioned to the others to drop to a walk, and the dust cloud settled around them. The adobe structure with its shaded portico and waist high wall that contained the rectangular courtyard with the gardens, was a welcome sight to the weary travelers. But as the Capitan sat his mount, leaning on the saddle horn with his elbow, talking with the friar, he glanced over his shoulder to motion for Diego to keep the men moving. Diego nodded, grinned and turned to tell the men, "We will be in a village by dark this night! Maybe we will have a meal cooked by a woman!"

The news met with many remarks as the men passed the news from one to another. The long column plodded on, every footfall raising a tuft of dust. Shortly after passing the mission, the trail took them to a river crossing and Diego halted the column to wait for the Capitan. The trees were thick and green on both sides, but more so on the far side. The men stepped down, led the horses to water and loosened the girths as they waited, many were seen stretching, bending backwards, and rubbing their rumps, tired of the hard-seated saddles. The water was murky, but the banks on both sides showed gravel and the crossing was well-used. When Capitan Almeida came near, he ordered, "Move out! We have much to do before we can stop!" and unexpectedly nudged his mount into the water to lead the way. Diego was surprised to see the Capitan take the lead, usually he would send someone ahead to be certain the crossing was safe, but Diego just shook his head, tightened the girth on the saddle and swung aboard, motioning the men to follow.

The first sight of the village was a lighted window in the dim light of dusk. The terrain was flat, the only break in the monotonous plodding was the sight of a cluster of tree cholla or a thicket of sage. And the welcome sight of the lighted window lifted the spirits of the weary travelers. Even the horses quickened their step as they drew near the scattered flat roofed adobe structures. Although they had passed several pueblos of the Tiwa and others, the sight of houses and a church spoke of civilization and people that spoke the same language.

The Capitan stopped the cavalcade before they reached the town plaza, motioning to a small adobe with a big corral attached, "We will put our animals there. Each man will roll out his bedroll behind the building and we will not go into the plaza until after daylight!"

"But Capitan, the men are hungry and thirsty, surely there is a cantina where we can refresh ourselves. It has been a long journey and there is much further to go, they need this, mi Capitan!" pleaded Diego.

De Almeida paused, shaking his head, glanced to the men then condescended, "Very well. But there is to be no disturbance! We will resupply early and leave. Any man that is not ready or tries to leave, will be shot!" He slapped his leg with his quirt and stomped away, determined to separate himself from what he considered to be rabble. He walked into the plaza that was laid out in the traditional Spanish villa style: a central plaza surrounded by buildings of all manner, most with a covered boardwalk. On the north side, an impressive church stood watch over the burgeoning community. With twin bell towers, and a cruciform outline, the structure was the most impressive of all in the village. As the Capitan neared, he noted a sign that told it to be the *San Felipe de Neri Church.*

A voice that came from beside him said, "This church has been here most of a hundred years. We of the Franciscan order have followed in the footsteps of Fray Manuel Moreno, one of the original founders of Alburquerque. I am Father Fernando Dominguez. May I be of help to you?"

The capitan nodded, "I am Capitan Francisco de Almeida, commanding an expedition to the northern mountains and the territory beyond the Sangre de Cristos." He paused, looked from the friar to the church, "It is a beautiful building, and unexpected here in this wild country."

"Yes, it is beautiful. The first building that was built in 1706 fell into disrepair and the roof had caved in, but we began to rebuild almost a decade ago and this is the result. However, there is still much to do, our work is never finished."

With another glance at the church, de Almeida turned away, "You will excuse me?" he said to the friar and started into the plaza. He needed to find a trading post to resupply and perhaps a place to refresh himself and spend the night. He spotted a long structure on the south end of the plaza with a long board sign that read *Cantina* and he knew he could find all his answers there, with a smile and a quick step, he walked across the plaza, his mouth watering at the thought of a good meal and some sangaree, or as some were calling the spiced wine, sangria.

12 / WIND RIVER

It was a familiar trail that Gabe took, the Shoshone village of Cougar's family behind them, and the mountains before them. He twisted in his saddle to get a last look at the rocky pinnacles of the mountains on the west side of the big lake, two or three prominent peaks standing above the rest but all showing jagged tips well above timberline. Gabe was reminded of a set of shark's teeth the captain of the ship that took them to England had shown him, the same sheer points that instilled a touch of fear at the sight of them. He turned back to face the stream that twisted through the grassy flats, they had traversed the boggy flats and now faced the stream. Cougar came beside him, nodded toward the water, "My people call that the Buffalo Fork of the Snake. The buffalo that migrate north, often come to this place." She leaned forward and looked to the east, "The smaller stream we follow is known as Blackrock Creek."

"I remember this place, and the creek yonder, and I've seen the black rock along the canyon. That's what we call basalt, it comes from volcanoes."

Cougar frowned, "What is . . . volcanoes?"

Gabe grinned, "That's kinda hard to explain, but I'll try." He paused, looked at the stream and said, "Let's cross over, then I'll tell you." He nudged Ebony forward, glanced back at the big grey pack horse that was running free rein, and rocked in his saddle as the big black tip toed down the bank and into the water. Another glance back showed the grey following, and Gabe lifted his feet from the stirrups, but the water didn't reach Ebony's belly. The river was about two hundred feet across, shallow all the way. They moved across the gravelly bottom easily and soon mounted the far bank where Gabe reined up to watch the others cross. Bobcat leaned around his father to watch Cougar and Fox come from the water, and as he tugged at Gabe's sleeve he asked, "Will we do that again?"

Gabe chuckled, "Prob'ly, but not too many times. There are other streams we might cross though." He twisted to look down at his son, "Why? Did you like that?"

"Ummhmm. I saw some fish too!" he declared, pointing to the water.

Cougar stopped beside them and said, "Volcanoes?"

Gabe lifted his head in a nod, grinning, then looked around. "I can't see it from here, but I'll point it out as we get near. Do you remember times when you felt the earth move, tremble and maybe roar?"

"You mean like it does where the water shoots high?"

"Yeah, like that. The reason the water shoots high is because way down deep in the earth, the rocks and such are all molten, or melted like fat in the fire, and when water hits it, it boils over and shoots up." He looked at Cougar's expression to see if she was understanding, and continued, just as Ezra and Dove came near. "Well, sometimes the hot molten rock also boils up and when it does it pushes up the dirt until it blows the top off, then shoots that hot rock everywhere, and some just flows down the side of the hill like water, but it's molten, or melted rock. Then after a time, it cools off and looks just like that black rock along the creek yonder." Cougar and Dove frowned, looking to one another and to the men, trying to discern if they were being truthful, then Cougar asked, "Does that happen many times?"

"It has, but mostly long, long ago. We've seen many places where it happened and the next time we come to such a place, we'll show you!" declared Gabe, looking at Ezra who nodded in agreement. Gabe pointed to the trail with his chin and gigged the black to the path, motioning Cougar to side him. The trail was wide and easy as they crossed the willow flats, in less than five miles they passed the confluence of the Buffalo and Blackrock, following the trail beside Blackrock creek. The trail gradually rose above the creek, traversing the shoulder of the wide timbered mesa that flanked the line of mountains that Gabe remembered held a long ridge of granite cliffs that hung well back and above the trail they followed.

As they crested the mesa, the trail twisted through the thicker timber, weaving in and out, but always near the shoulder that sided the creek below. It was nearing mid-day when the trail flanked the high mountains and a green valley opened before them. Below them in the shallow valley, Blackrock creek meandered and twisted snake-like through the tall grass. A small herd of elk lifted their heads at the intruders and trotted off, disappearing into a cut that would take them to higher country. Gabe looked down at Wolf, "That's prob'ly cuz o' you, boy. They got a whiff of wolf and decided to go to the timber."

Gabe looked back at the others, "What say we go down by the creek and have us somethin' to eat?"

"I'm all for that," chimed Ezra, nudging his big bay to the grassy flat. The others readily followed, and they soon had a small fire going and the horses were enjoying the graze. Soon back on the trail, another eight or nine miles brought them to the crest of the mountain pass that split two snow crested granite peaks. The cool wind prompted the riders to shuck into their capotes and blankets for the youngsters. Once they topped the pass, the view took in the long range of the Wind River Mountains, prompting the travelers to stop and enjoy the scenery. Dove looked below the trail, pointing with her chin, "The Wind River," to the headwaters of a small stream that coursed its way through the timbered foothills, chuckling its way to the lower climes. Cougar rode the spotted rump appaloosa mare and its colt romped beside her. Cougar had started calling the mare, Mama, since that was how Gabe often referred to the mare and her colt. Although Cougar still led the steeldust mustang pack horse and Dove trailed the buckskin, the big grey that followed Gabe and the mule that followed Ezra both trailed free rein.

The frisky colt had become a little adventurous and would often run away from the others, usually chasing after Wolf, and would occasionally go exploring into the trees or along the river bottom. The trail had just bent around a bit of a knob when the view of a long granite crested ridge rose high above the timber in the valley below. Appearing as a parade of soldiers marching shoulder to shoulder, the massive formation of grey pinnacles was spellbinding. Gabe reined up, nodded toward the ridge, and shook his head, words unnecessary. He rested one elbow on the pommel of the saddle and leaned forward, taking in the view, enjoying the majesty of the Creator. But his enjoyment was short-lived and was broken by the unmistakable scream of a mountain lion. All the horses balked, side-stepping, heads up and eyes glaring. The riders grabbed reins and manes to keep their seats.

Gabe looked in the direction of the scream, heard the cough of the terror of the timber, and snatched his rifle from the scabbard. Standing in the stirrups, he searched the tree line when the spotted rump colt burst from the trees, long gangly legs propelling the scared yearling as it ran toward its mother. No more than two yards behind, the tawny coat of the catamount showing rippling muscles as long claws dug into the grass as it stretched out in pursuit of the tasty colt. Gabe brought the Ferguson to his shoulder, held Ebony still with his legs as he spoke, "Easy boy, easy," and swung the rifle to follow the cougar then squeezed off his shot. The big rifle barked its authoritative roar and spat smoke into the spring greenery. The puma of the peaks tumbled with the impact of the .65 caliber ball striking it just behind the shoulder. He had no sooner rolled into the grass than the black wolf leaped on the cat. The cougar snarled, spat, and lay still with Wolf, his teeth buried in the back of the neck, snapping the head side to side.

Gabe shouted, "Wolf! Here!" and watched the big black wolf turn, mouth wide and bloody teeth showing, and with another glance at the cougar, he trotted back to the side of Ebony and Gabe. Cougar Woman scowled at the colt as it stood trembling at the side of his mother, then leaned forward to see some deep gouges in the rump of the colt. As she slipped from the saddle, she told Gabe, "We'll need to tend to him," nodding toward the colt. She went to her saddle bags, put a hand on Fox's leg and said, "You sit still there. I'll be back." By the time she dug out her pouch with the wilderness medicines, Gabe had a rope around the neck of the still trembling colt and was stroking his neck and talking to him.

Cougar had fashioned a salve from the sticky red resin on the fresh leaf shoots of the aspen, combining it with a few other of her mysterious ingredients and making a soothing salve. She stepped to the side of the colt, wiped the blood from the gouges from the claws of the cougar, and applied her salve. The colt twitched his hide at her touch, but did not spook, turning to look at Cougar as she soothed his wounds. Only three of the gouges were deep, the rest were but scratches and she looked at those on the left rump, then said to Gabe, "I think you'll find the cougar had an injury to his front paw. Only one of these marks show a long claw."

"Well, Ezra went to get the hide, so he'll be back shortly and tell us. He'll probably get the claws too."

Cougar looked at the colt's rump, checked him for

any other wounds, knowing a cougar would often try to use its teeth to take down a quarry, but the colt showed no other injuries. She went back to her saddle bags and replaced the pouch of remedies, "Baby hurt?" asked Fox, frowning.

"Yes he was. But he will be alright soon," answered Cougar, stepping aboard the appy and pulling Fox close against her.

They looked up as Ezra came back, the hide of the cougar rolled up tight, flesh side out to try to limit the smell of the cat to keep the horses from spooking. But they caught the smell anyway, sidestepping a little and looking at Ezra wide-eyed, but he spoke and reassured them as he stuffed the hide into the pannier aboard the mule. "He was an old one! Had a few scars on him, but the hide'll be alright. I didn't take the claws, too much trouble and didn't have 'em all anyway."

Cougar glanced at Gabe and saw him nod, grinning. "Yeah, Cougar said he'd be injured or somethin'. Didn't have enough claws to bring the colt down. Course that's a good thing for us I reckon." He gigged Ebony to the trail and started into the wide valley of the headwaters of the Wind River. They had traveled less than two or three miles when Gabe reined up and pointed to the south of the trail and said, "See there! That butte atop the mesa yonder, where all that reddish black rock is? That's the remains of a volcano, like I told you. And all those patches of black rock, that's the lava it spat out when it erupted!"

The others shaded their eyes as they looked and Cougar asked, "When did that happen?"

"I wouldn't know. But it was a long time ago, that's for certain!"

Gabe pushed on down the trail, looking for a likely place to camp for the night. If they made good time, they would probably reach the summer camp of the Kuccuntikka Shoshone sometime tomorrow, and the family of Dove would have some time to visit with their grandchildren.

13 / CAMP

The trail dropped from the higher ranges and sided the rim rock drop-off of a long mesa that guided them into the valley of the Wind River. Although the head-waters twisted through a narrow valley, the foothills on the east lay like a green blanket over the rolling foothills that pointed to the granite tipped peaks of the Wind River range. This had been home country for Gabe and Ezra, the land of the Shoshone where they spent their second winter in the mountains and where they met the sisters, Pale Otter and Grey Dove that would become their wives. It was later when Otter was killed by a jealous rival, a warrior that had become an outcast and enemy of the people and in his blind resentment and possessiveness, captured and killed the wife of Spirit Bear, or Gabe.

Grey Dove was anxious to see her family and let her mother and father know the children, Chipmunk and Squirrel. Although they had known Chipmunk in his early years, that was before Squirrel was born and before Chipmunk had grown into the rambunctious and curious boy that he was today. Ezra and Dove could not be prouder of their little ones, and that joy and delight continually showed in the eyes of the proud parents.

The trail turned to the southeast, paralleling the tips of the many timbered finger ridges that came from the high up mountains. On the north of the river, flat-top mesas showing layers of red rock that showed like stripes on the bottom of the skirts of the buttes. Tall grasses waved in the breeze, herds of elk, some showing velvet nubbins that would grow into massive antlers, grazed near the river, unconcerned with the passersby. Antelope, with their prong horns and white rumps and bellies, stood atop the mesas and watched the intruders following the trail below. Tall cottonwoods and burr oak stood proudly along the banks of the river and mule deer lifted their heads, curious of the visitors, but not interested enough to interrupt their munching of the luscious grasses on the river bank.

It was a peaceful and pleasant time, riding under the cloudless blue sky, warm sun making the colors of creation stand boldly before them, as Gabe looked at Cougar Woman, "If I didn't know better, I'd think we were the only people in the world!"

Cougar smiled, "We are the only people in *our* world!"

Gabe nodded, then noticed a fox chasing a cottontail, weaving in and out among the grasses and the sagebrush, only to be disappointed when the bunny disappeared down a hole. The fox tried digging, but soon gave up and Gabe chuckled, pointing to the fox with his chin, "Guess he's gonna go hungry for a while, even if he is in *our* world!"

The river moved away from the finger ridges, butting up against the rimrock buttes on the north side forcing the travelers to cross over. They chose a spot where the river made a wide bend back on itself, leaving a broad island in the middle and a shallow crossing below. The current was easy, the water no more than a couple feet deep, and the gravel bar offered good footing. Gabe nodded for Cougar to take the lead, the colt splashing beside its mother on the downstream side. They made an easy crossing and the others followed in her wake. Once across, the trail sided the river, but the meandering and twisting river prompted Gabe to look for a place to camp for the night. A small stream came from the south side, cascading off the bluff and appearing to come from around a point of land that piqued Gabe's curiosity. He looked to Cougar, "You wait here, I'm gonna check this stream and hill up here, might be a good place for the night."

He motioned Wolf ahead and gigged Ebony to a trot to climb the slight slope overlooking the cascading creek. His suspicion proved out and he spotted a narrow valley with a crystalline lake lying between the bluffs with a wide grassy park just below. He stood in his stirrups, turned around and waved the others to follow. Gabe looked down at Bobcat and said, "Looks like we found us a nice camp for the night, boy, whatchu think?"

Bobcat yawned, looked at his father, "I tired."

Gabe chuckled, answered, "Me too, son, me too."

Within moments, the others were beside him and looked where he pointed, each pleased and surprised to see the turquoise gem of a lake that invited them to camp. Ezra said, "Bet there's some nice trout in there!"

"Have at it, my friend. You catch 'em, we'll eat 'em," answered Gabe, gigging Ebony to the faint trail that took the high side above the creek. The upper end of the lake held a wide grassy flat that suited the group for their camp and they quickly had everything in place and the cookfire started. Ezra had disappeared to the inlet, spotting another adjoining lake that lay no more than fifty yards above the first one, prompting him to use the adjoining stream for his fishing. The terrain all about was thick with sagebrush, scattered juniper and piñon, an occasional spruce or fir that stretched higher than the juniper, and the hillsides above the lake were littered with lichen covered boulders and rockpiles.

As Gabe sat above the lake, he looked back at the distant Absaroka range of mountains, and the lowering sun that was painting the few wispy clouds with the broad brush of brilliant gold and orange. He was on the slope above the lake, sitting above a short stretch of rimrock that held a couple of big junipers, and he watched the ripples on the lake catch and pass on the lances of color from the western sunset. He stood and started back to camp when something on the back side of a boulder caught his eye and he stepped closer for a better look. He dropped to one knee and touched the image on the rock, an ancient petroglyph that portrayed two hunters, three buffalo and an antelope, and another hunter driving the animals toward the two others. He grinned, seeing the crude carving on stone, probably etched decades if not a century or more before they came to this place. The warriors held bows and arrows, one with a lance, and the bison and antelope were unmistakable by the horns and humps. Someone had hunted and camped in this very place, so many years ago.

He grinned, stood, and with Wolf at his side, walked back to camp. Cougar looked up at her man, saw his expression, and asked, "And what did you see?"

"We are not the first to camp here," he declared. "Someone was here, long ago, and told of hunting and camping here. He left us a message on the rock up there," nodding to the hillside where the petroglyph resided. The women frowned, looked at him with a question written on their face and Gabe told them of the petroglyph he found. He glanced at the sky and the dim light of dusk, and said, "If you want to see it, I'll stay here with the little ones."

The women looked at one another, smiled and nodded. Gabe glanced at the four youngsters, the two older boys snoozing and the younger pair playing, then turned and pointed out where the carving was, "It's on the back side," he explained. They nodded and started up the slope, anxious to see the message from the past. Gabe sat beside the fire, saw the coffee pot at the side of the fire and the biscuits baking in the dutch oven that sat nearby and covered with hot coals. He shrugged as he realized they were waiting for Ezra to return with some trout and he thought, *I sure hope he doesn't disappoint!* then poured himself a cup of coffee and sat back, enjoying the cool of the evening.

Ezra returned before the women and looked around, looked at Gabe and without asking, questioned the whereabouts of the women with his expression. Gabe chuckled, "They're up on the hill yonder lookin' at a petroglyph I found."

"Oh, what was it?" asked Ezra, stripping eight nice trout from the forked willow he used to carry them.

"Pictured three warriors, some buffalo and antelope. Looked old."

"Ummm, so, does that mean you're cookin'?"

"No. But I'll help you clean 'em and pack 'em in mud," offered Gabe. They walked to the water's edge and quickly cleaned the fish, packing each one in mud to bake them in the coals, and, returned to the fire to put the mudded fish into the coals, and cover them over.

The women returned, smiled when they saw their muddy men, and laughed. Dove said, "You two need to wash. We'll finish this," she ordered, nodding at the fire and their meal.

The men grinned, looking at one another, and went to water's edge to wash up. They were squatting, their toes almost touching the water, and dipping their hands in the water, when Wolf growled, looking to the low end of the lake. The men stopped, looked in the same direction and in the dim light of dusk, made out the figures of three riders, following their tracks from below, up to this lake. As they watched, the men stopped, one motioning toward them, and Gabe said, "Prob'ly saw our fire."

"Yeah, didn't expect that, bein' up here and away from the trail. They musta seen our tracks and decided to follow."

"Let's get our rifles," stated Gabe, glancing around. "You take the high ground, up there above the rim by those trees. I'll stay close to the fire and the women'll take the young'uns into the rocks, yonder."

When they returned to the fire and explained about the visitors, Cougar said, "I'll go with Dove and the children, but I will come back."

"Not unless I call for you."

She scowled at her man, snatched up the youngsters and followed Dove into the rocks.

14 / ABSÁALOOKE

Gabe kept his eyes away from the fire and his impatience got to him, forcing him to climb the rocky rise behind the camp for a look see toward where they saw the three riders. He was about half way up the rise, when he turned for a quick look, just in time to see the three separate, two returning the way they came, but one slowly starting up the trail toward their camp. Gabe knew Ezra was watching and probably would come to the same conclusion he had, but he used the call of the night hawk to signal his friend. Using a pattern they had developed between them, he let Ezra know the riders had split, but one was coming. Another cry of the nighthawk, used when their nest was threatened and sounded like the 'chirp chirp' of a smaller bird, told Ezra he believed they were coming to the camp. The two men had been together through so many challenges, they thought alike, and Gabe was certain Ezra knew what he was thinking now.

The scope was useless in the dim light, but Gabe's eyesight was accustomed to the pale light of the moon and watched as the lone rider stopped near a distant juniper and tethered his mount. Gabe thought, *He's doing exactly what I would do, comin' on foot, quiet like, thinking he can get close and scout us out for the others. Well, if he wants to play that game . . .* Gabe went closer to where the women and children were and quietly called to them. "Come on out, we gotta play hide and seek with these visitors."

The women came, each with their two children, the little ones asleep on their shoulders. Cougar looked at her man, "Who are they?"

"Not sure. They didn't get too close, but one thinks he sneakin' up on us to scout us out for the others, so, we'll make it look like we'd be easy pickin's." As they made their way back to camp, Gabe continued to explain about the others and that he believed they went to fetch the rest of the hunting party. "We'll let this one see us, all family like. Then after he leaves, we'll set a trap for 'em."

A deep-throated call from the nighthawk told Gabe the scout was near, and he motioned to the women to make busy. The smaller children were asleep on the blankets under the trees, but the older two were near Gabe. He leaned back, sipping on his coffee, acting as nonchalant as possible, watching the boys as they jumped up to chase a little lizard. There were several tall fir trees that lined out on the lake shore at the base of the slope where Ezra was hidden, his promontory giving a full view of the trees and the slope that held the narrow trail. He watched the scout flit from tree to tree, crouch beside the one nearest the camp, and watch the activity of the camp. If he was as good as he should be, he would count the horses and the number in the camp, getting some indication if all were present in the camp, or elsewhere. Ezra had picketed his bay further away and out of sight for that very reason.

After a few moments, the scout was satisfied and skulked away, and when far enough from the camp, he broke into a trot to return to his horse. Ezra watched as the man swung aboard and started back down the trail. A quick glance to the sky showed the rising moon, and Ezra grinned, knowing he and Gabe fought well in the dark. Where the rider took to the trail, it was too dark and too far to see, but in a short while, he heard the scuffling and clatter of horses' hooves, but they soon stopped near the same cluster of trees where the scout had tethered his mount.

Ezra waited, squinting and staring, trying to determine the number of the party, and counted about a dozen. He cupped his hands and using the code of the nighthawk, with the high-pitched peent and the low throated booms that followed, told Gabe of twelve visitors. A quick chirp of the nest-threatened nighthawk, told Ezra that Gabe understood. Gabe looked to Cougar and Dove, "Dove, you and the youngsters move into the trees on the far side of the horses. They won't shoot toward the horses for fear of hitting them, and you'll be safe. But take your rifle anyway and keep one eye on that creek behind you. I don't think they'll try that, the slope yonder is too steep, but . . ."

Dove chuckled, "Have you known me to be without my rifle?"

Gabe shook his head, grinning. He looked at Cougar, nodded to the slope behind the camp, "There's a big boulder up there. You cover the camp from there. I'll be near that snag yonder, that puts me 'bout half way between you and Ezra. Have you got your pistol?"

"Yes. But I prefer my bow instead of the rifle."

"That's fine. You just keep any of 'em away from the horses and kids. That creek that feeds the lake will keep any of 'em from tryin' that way, so I think they'll be coming from the trail and the edge of the lake, behind those trees yonder."

Within just a few moments, everyone was in place with Wolf beside Cougar Woman. The half-moon had risen enough to paint the surrounding hills with that pale blue of night that betrayed shadows, especially moving shadows. When the warriors approached, the narrow trail behind the trees forced them into a single line, but once past the trees, they fell under the sights of Ezra perched above the trail on the line of rust colored rimrock and the few cedars that clung tightly to the rocky ledge.

Gabe watched as four warriors separated from the others, coming toward Gabe's perch and the upper end of the camp. Four others spaced themselves out along the edge of the trail, while the others had stayed in the trees, below the camp and near the water. To the north edge of the camp, the thick trees held the picketed horses, and Dove and the children beyond. The warriors were coming from the west along the lake shore, the south beneath Ezra, and the east below Gabe and Cougar. Suddenly the entire band started a stealthy stalk, moving closer to the camp where the fire still burned, bedrolls were lain out and stuffed with whatever would make them look occupied, and nothing moved.

Suddenly Cougar Woman called out, in the Crow tongue, "Are the Absáalooke such cowards they have to sneak into a camp of women and children?"

Gabe was startled and looked toward Cougar who stood atop the boulder, shouting to the attackers. Her shout had stopped the movement of the warriors until one answered, "Who dares to call the great warriors of the Absáalooke cowards! Show yourself!"

"I am here! Or are you blind also?" challenged Cougar Woman. "I am Cougar Woman, war leader of the Tukkutikka Shoshone! And my warriors are all around you! I am with the great warriors, Black Buffalo and Spirit Bear, friends of the Absáalooke war leader, Spotted Crow, and his chief, No Intestines. Would you dare attack the friends of your leaders?"

"They are not our leaders! We are of the Eelalapito band of the Absáalooke. Our chief is Red Calf, and I am the war leader, Buffalo Tongue! Will you fight? Or talk us to death? Or invite us to your fire to talk like friends?"

"Show yourself and I will answer!" declared Cougar Woman, watching the warriors on the slope below her and looking to the trees by the shoreline where the speaker stood in the shadows.

One man stepped forward, and at his motion, three more came from the trees behind him. At his signal, the four below the trail stood, then those on the slope below Cougar and Gabe stood. Cougar responded, "Go to the fire, we will join you."

Cougar looked at Gabe, grinning as he shook his head, and when he joined her, they walked to the camp together, Wolf at their side. When they entered the firelight, several of the warriors stepped back at the sight of the big wolf, then looked at Gabe and Cougar Woman, wide-eyed as Gabe called to Wolf, and he stood at the side of Gabe, looking at each of the warriors as if he was looking at a menu in the wilderness restaurant. Gabe spoke softly, "Easy boy, easy now. Stay with me."

"I have heard of a white warrior with a black wolf that has fought with the Mountain Crow against the Blackfoot. Are you the one they have spoken of around the fires?"

"Mebbe, dunno. Haven't been around their fires lately. But we," nodding to Cougar Woman, and toward Ezra who stood just at the edge of firelight, having come up behind the warriors, unseen and un-heard, "have fought with our Crow brothers against the Blackfoot."

When Gabe motioned toward Ezra and the war-riors turned to see the dark-skinned man behind them, they were startled and stepped aside for Ezra to enter the camp. He walked toward Gabe, stood be-side him with Wolf between them, and turned to face the warriors. He nodded toward the fire, "I reckon those fish are 'bout ready." He looked at Gabe, "You hungry? Cuz I shore am!" He spoke in the tongue of the Shoshone, a language understood by many of the Crow. He looked at the leader of the band, "Wasn't expecting company, but we'll share what we have!" nodding to the fire.

At the invitation, everyone seemed to relax, weap-ons were laid aside, but kept near, and two men dis-appeared into the darkness, dispatched by their leader to bring their horses with their day's kill to the camp. Soon, there were two fires, meat sizzling over both, and conversations were springing up among them all. In short order, the group talked and laughed as if they had been friends a long time. The two older children ran and scampered among the warriors, some of whom played with them, probably fathers in their own right, and the meal was shared and enjoyed. When everyone turned in, Gabe noted the Crow had stationed a guard near their horses, and Gabe quietly spoke to Ezra, "I don't want it to be obvious, but I reckon we need our own guard tonight, ya reckon?"

"Ummhmm. They been real friendly like, but I've also noticed a few of 'em lookin' at our packs, horses, and women. Ain't nothin' in these mountains to keep 'em from wantin' to take everything we got and skedaddle!"

"Exactly what I was thinkin'." He paused for a moment, considering, "There's a point yonder, just above the trees, that has a good view of the camp an' such, and we could see, and not be seen. You know, just in case."

"You wanna go first?" asked Ezra, looking at his friend and glancing toward the bedrolls.

"Sure, I'll go first. And unless I miss my guess, Cougar will wanna take a turn. So, I'll wake her, you can take the last watch. And we'll leave Wolf with you."

Ezra nodded and went to his blankets beside Dove and crawled in beside her. The children lay on the far side, sound asleep, and Dove just mumbled something unintelligible and rolled over.

Gabe explained to Cougar what they planned, and she nodded, "It is good. I believe Buffalo Tongue is a good man, but what we have, horses, packs, and family, would be riches to most warriors and hard to resist."

"Yup. And if I was one o' them, I'd sure want to make a try for you!" he chuckled.

"That's because they do not know me! But no warrior wants to crawl in the blankets with a proven war leader, except you!" she grinned.

Gabe picked up his rifle, felt at his waist for his pistol, stuffed a saddle pistol in his belt, and started for the trees. They were far enough from the sleeping Crow that he could easily move into the trees, unseen and unheard. Within moments, he had mounted the outcropping and seated himself just behind a big boulder, but within view of the camp and the sleeping Crow. Wolf lay beside him, also looking at the camp, but with his muzzle between his paws and his tail curled around his rump. But Gabe had confidence in his friend, knowing Wolf would hear and see any danger long before he could.

15 / ASSAULT

Cougar moved stealthily up to the outcropping where Gabe sat with Wolf. She had been too restless and could not sleep, knowing it was about time for her to relieve Gabe, she climbed the slope to sit with him for a short while. Wolf lifted his head when he sensed her near, beating his tail against the ground and telling Gabe she was coming. He looked back along the narrow trail and watched her emerge from the dark timber, her smile showing in the darkness. She slipped up close to him and sat, her hand on his knee as he whispered, "Nothing moving yet, but I've got that feeling that something will happen soon."

"I know, and that they are so close." She looked at Gabe, "You should get some rest. If I see anything, I will give the call of the magpie."

Gabe nodded, looking toward the camp of the Crow. They had picketed their horses near the trail, and their bedrolls were on the upper end of the grassy flat, about thirty or forty yards from the camp of Gabe and company. While the Crow were in the open, Gabe's party was just inside the tree line, and the cluster of fir and juniper showed black in the night. "If they try anything, it'll be soon, and I'm guessing they'll either move near the shoreline, or along this upper end and drop into the trees. Either way, as long as the moon," looking up at the glowing orb high above, "isn't blocked by clouds, you should easily see them."

She smiled at her man's need of explaining the obvious to her but nodded in understanding as he stood to leave. They stood together, embracing, until he pulled away to go to their camp. As Cougar took his warmed-up seat on the rock, she watched her man disappear into the darkness. She reached down and stroked the scruff of Wolf and he pushed closer to her, then turned to watch the camp.

Elk that Walks and Goes Ahead were two warriors of the Absáalooke that were known for their appetite for women. Although Goes Ahead had a woman and a child, Elk that Walks had lost his woman to the sickness of the white man traders and her absence filled him with both a bitterness against the white man and a hunger for another woman. The two men had exchanged glances while they ate and watched the Shoshone women that were joined to these two strangers. They drew aside and talked with Elk that Walks suggesting, "We could easily take them in the night when they sleep. If you take the dark one, I will take the white man. We can slit their throats and take the women and children for our own, or just kill the children and take the women and their rifles."

"I do not think it will be so easy to do. I have heard the stories of these men, how they fought against the Blackfoot."

"In the dark, we can take them without a fight!" snarled Elk that Walks. "Are you afraid?"

"No! What of the others? They will want what is in the packs and more!"

"We will have the women and the horses! That big black stallion is mine!"

"When?" asked Goes Ahead.

"I will wake you. It will be after the moon is high."

Cougar lifted her eyes to the sky, noting the high point of the bright moon just over half, the unhindered brilliance of the stars. She looked at the milky way or what the natives referred to as the Path to the Other side and smiled at the memories of the many times she and Gabe had sat and talked about the heavens. Her attention was brought back to the present when a low growl came from Wolf as he lifted his head and came to his feet, looking in the direction of the Crow camp. Cougar moved her eyes across the camp, knowing she would see as much and more with her peripheral vision as with a direct stare. One shadow moved at the upper end of the camp, went to his knees and another moved.

Cougar cupped her hands, faced the camp of her family, and gave the yak-yak-yak call of the magpie. She reached down to Wolf and ran her fingers through his scruff as she leaned close and said, "Watch 'em boy." She nocked an arrow, keeping her eyes on the camp, and saw the two shadows move above the camp of the Crow and start along the upper edge of the grassy flat, near the rock and sage strewn slope where she was concealed. No others were rousing.

Gabe came instantly awake at the call of the magpie, recognizing it as Cougar's warning. He rolled from his blankets, stuffed a pistol in his belt and grabbed his rifle. A quick glance across the way showed Ezra also readying himself. Each man stepped into the trees, yet stayed close to their sleeping families, watching over the still forms. Gabe looked through the low boughs of the fir, looking toward the moonlit grassy flat and the Crow camp beyond. He moved enough to look to the hillside, believing any attackers would stay near the edge of the grass and use the backdrop of the hill to mask their approach. Dropping to one knee, he bent low to look below the lowest branch and saw movement.

The two Crow warriors picked their way stealthily in the dim moonlight, moving above their camp and following the edge of the grassy flat where it ended at the base of the rocky hillside. They could easily move quietly in the grass, but to traverse the rock-strewn slope with cactus and sage and loose rocks would not be so easy. Elk that Walks moved in a crouch, knife in hand, anticipating his attack on the white man. Yet any plan made by man that involves other men or animals, is always subject to failure. But the two warriors, like so many with villainous thoughts that devised devious ways to harm and rob others, believed their plan would not fail. Their measured breathing matched their stealth as they neared the trees.

Cougar stood above them, following the two with her bow, waiting to release her arrow, and with a nudge of her knee, Wolf launched himself from the boulder and Cougar loosed her arrow. The arrow took the warrior in the lead, burying itself in his side to the fletching. Almost at the same instant, Wolf struck the second warrior, bearing him to the ground, his teeth buried in the man's neck and throat. Growling and snarling, he shook his head side to side, ripping the man's throat and neck, stifling his screams.

Elk that Walks had been driven to his knees by the impact of the arrow. He grabbed at the shaft; eyes wide as he struggled. He fell forward catching himself with his left hand, his right grasping the arrow as he fought for air. As he fell forward, he saw the moccasined feet before him, then rolled to his side to look up into the glaring stare of the white man, Spirit Bear.

Gabe looked at Wolf, now astraddle of his victim, and called his friend to his side, "Here boy, c'mere," as he slapped his pants leg.

Cougar came near, another arrow nocked and looking at the two downed warriors. With a glance to Gabe she said, "The others have not moved," nodding back toward the other Crow.

"I'll drag these over there," motioning with his head to the rockpile near the tree line, "but you need to watch for the others. I don't think they'll be so happy with this," nodding toward the downed warriors.

Ezra had come from the trees and added, "Yeah. I'm thinkin' we might wanna pack up and leave even 'fore they do."

Gabe looked at his friend, frowning, "You might be right. But if it comes to a fight, we would be at a disadvantage if we were running away."

"But if it's a fight here, they have us outnumbered three to one."

"Yeah," replied Gabe, then looked to Cougar, "What do you think?"

"It would be good to leave. If they come after, we can set up an ambush. But we cannot leave without them knowing."

"Yeah, but if we're mounted and ready by the time they realize what we're doin', that might give us enough of a lead to get where we want. But I'm thinkin' we need to tell Buffalo Tongue what happened," responded Gabe.

Ezra said, "So, do we pack up or not?"

Gabe glanced to Cougar, then back to Ezra, "Yeah, get started. I'll join you just as soon as I get these two," motioning to the dead Crow, "outta the way." He looked at Cougar, "Wolf can stay with me, you help Ezra and I'll be along." She nodded, and the two quickly disappeared into the trees.

Although it was customary for the dead to be stripped of their weapons and more, Gabe left the two bodies undisturbed. He lay them beside one another and left to join his friends as they readied to leave. He shook his head as he thought, *Here's hopin' we can get outta here in one piece!*

They hurriedly packed up and saddled up, moving quietly as possible, but the movement alone disturbed the stillness of the night. Gabe lifted Fox to Cougar as she sat the appaloosa, and lifted Bobcat to his saddle. He jammed his foot in the stirrup to swing aboard the black when Wolf growled and prompted Gabe to turn around to see Buffalo Tongue and another warrior walking toward them.

"I see you are leaving; it is early for traveling," commented Buffalo Tongue.

Gabe noticed the man had his hand on the toma-hawk that was in his sash, and he stood as if expecting an attack. The man beside him, Yellowtail, held his tomahawk at his side, glaring at the family. Gabe faced the war leader, "That's right. But we had a little trouble with a couple of your men and thought it best to leave before more tried something."

Buffalo Tongue scowled, glanced at Yellowtail, "What happened?"

"They're over there, by those rocks," stated Gabe, pointing toward the edge of the trees. "Two of them thought they'd take us in the night but were mistaken. We're not so easy to kill as they thought."

Buffalo Tongue motioned to his companion to go to the bodies, then looked at Gabe, "Was there a fight? We heard nothing."

"One was taken by Cougar Woman," nodding to Cougar aboard the appaloosa, "with an arrow as he neared our camp, knife in hand. Wolf took the other one."

Buffalo Tongue frowned as he looked down at the black wolf that stood beside the man. Yellowtail returned, scowling, and showing his anger, "They have killed Elk that Walks and Goes Ahead!" He turned to look at Gabe, his eyes showing anger and lust for vengeance.

Buffalo Tongue looked at Gabe, "I am not surprised they are the ones that did this. They were wrong.

You had opened your camp to us, shared a meal with us, and should not have been attacked." He paused, looked at Yellowtail and back to Gabe, "Go in peace."

Yellowtail quickly turned to look at his war leader and started to argue, but the uplifted hand of the man stilled his argument. Buffalo Tongue watched as Gabe swung aboard his black and nudged the mount forward to lead his group from the camp. He looked at his fellow warrior, shook his head and motioned him back to their camp. He watched as Yellowtail stomped away, growling as he left.

16 / AMBUSH

Gabe led them through the trees to cross the creek that flowed from the higher lake to the lower. It was wide and shallow but cascaded over the rocks with a quick drop to the lower lake and in the dim moonlight, Ebony paused, dropped his head for a close look and at the urging of Gabe, slowly picked his way across. It was less than a hundred fifty feet across, the horses' hooves clattering among the rocks and riffles of the stream, but they were soon on dry ground on the far side. With a glance over his shoulder, Gabe saw the others easily crossing and turned to mentally chart their course over the long ridge and into the valley of the Wind River. With no trail to follow, he let Ebony have his head and pick his own path, occasionally urging him to angle up the long ridge and they soon crossed over. They paused, took a long look at the vast land that stretched before them, but with the meandering river in the bottom showing like a huge black snake in the moonlight, Gabe gigged Ebony to move off the long slope toward the river below.

The barren slope showed bright in the moonlight, the only obstacles a few patches of sage or cacti, but the long descent was easily traversed and within less than three miles, they were at the side of the Wind River. Gabe paused, waited for the others to catch up and as Cougar came alongside, "We'll keep moving. I wanna put some distance between us and the Crow."

Cougar nodded, "The one called Yellowtail will seek vengeance." She spoke softly as to not cause Fox to stir, but she was somber as she spoke.

Ezra nudged his big bay alongside Gabe, "You think they'll follow?"

"Maybe not the entire party, but I'm thinkin' Yellowtail will try to get some to join him and come after us."

"Then let's get a move on!" declared Ezra, twisting in his saddle to look back up the slope they just descended.

"You take the lead. We'll just follow the trail by the river, I think it takes to the high flats after a spell, but basically follows the river. I'll watch our backtrail and after it gets light, I'll find a high point and scope the country behind us."

"I will stay with you," declared Cougar, her expression dissuading Gabe from objecting.

Gabe nodded, motioned for Ezra to lead off, and waited as the pack mule followed and Dove, leading the buckskin mare packhorse, passed. With a nod to Cougar, Gabe let her follow Dove and he nudged Ebony behind her steeldust mustang packhorse. Another five or six miles of the southeast bound trail brought them into a bit of a canyon as the slow rising sun shed more light on their trail. The beginning of daylight showed the valley with buttes on the north side boldly displaying wide bands of color between layers of rock, giving the impression of an artist's palette with the varying colors. Trees, mostly cottonwood, birch, and bur oak, sided the river, but the hillsides were all but barren, showing a little green wherever juniper, cedar and piñon found purchase. The valley bottom showed green with deep grass, but sage was prolific and crowded the grass, leaving only bunch grass in scattered flats.

A small rivulet joined the Wind from the south and a few yards further on, a good-sized creek joined from the north, adding to the flow of the Wind River as it pushed deeper into the canyon. After making a couple of dogleg bends, one to the right and one to the left, the river sided some tall red clay buttes that seemed to overhang the river like ochre giants waiting to pounce on any passersby. Gabe reined up where another little run-off creek split the buttes, prompting Cougar to stop and look back. He motioned to the cut, "I'm goin' up here, see if I can get on top of one of those buttes and have a look see."

Cougar nodded, reined her appaloosa around and followed Gabe into the narrow cut between the buttes. As they rounded the tall butte on the east side of the little creek, Gabe stopped, pointing to the butte, "I'll leave Ebony with you and climb that for a look around."

Cougar did not answer, but stepped down, standing Fox beside her and went to the side of Ebony to accept Bobcat as Gabe handed him down. Once the youngsters were seated on the grassy flat, Gabe tethered Ebony near the creek, letting him freely drink and graze, then with scope in hand, pistol in his belt, and rifle in the other hand, he started to the butte. He motioned for Wolf to stay with Cougar and the youngsters, then turned and started his climb. A slight trail took him behind the butte, where the slope offered easier access to the top. He angled his climb across the back face and soon crested out on top. As he hoped, the butte was high enough to offer an unhindered view of their backtrail and he bellied down to use the scope.

As he scanned the area, focusing mainly on their backtrail, he saw several antelope, a couple coyotes, three deer coming to water at river's edge, and an ambitious fox chasing a cottontail. But in the near reaches, there was no sign of anyone following. He moved the scope to focus on the more distant back-trail, to the northwest, and as he slowly searched, a bit of dust rose, catching his eye. He waited, focused again, and watched. Within moments, three riders showed on the trail that sided the river. He checked their location and guessed them to be about where the trail from the lakes met the river, or about six or seven miles behind them. A distance that could be covered in just over an hour. He looked again, making certain of his judgment, then slammed to scope down, put it in the case and took to his trail off the butte.

When he joined Cougar, she could tell by his expression they were followed. She asked, "How many?"

"I could only see three. Probably Yellowtail and a couple of his friends," answered Gabe as he handed Fox up to Cougar who now sat on the appaloosa, then handed her the lead rope of the steeldust. He swung Bobcat up atop Ebony and stepped aboard himself, whistled for the big grey pack horse to follow since he was following free rein.

Cougar asked, "How far?"

"Maybe an hour, or less. We need to catch up with Ezra and decide what we're gonna do."

"We cannot outrun them, we must stop and fight," declared Cougar, gigging the appy after the big grey.

"You're right about that. We just need to find the right spot."

When they broke from the close confines of the

canyon, Ezra and Dove waited by the river, their horses grazing and the children playing in the grass. When Ezra saw Gabe's expression, he motioned to Dove to get the little ones and he fetched the horses. "So, how many and how far?" he asked as he lifted Squirrel to Dove.

"Three, 'bout an hour."

Ezra swung Chipmunk to his seat behind the cantle of his saddle and stepped aboard himself. "We gonna stop and fight or . . .?"

"Soon as we find a good spot!" answered Gabe and kicked Ebony up to a canter. Cougar was close behind and Ezra and Dove followed. The string of eight horses lined out across the grass, following the river as it bent around a point and opened into a narrow valley, sided with long sage flats on the far side, and slope sided mesas on the near side. Gabe rode past a point where the near buttes pushed toward the river, making the narrow shoulder with the trail cut near the water. A quick glance to his right showed a narrow, but deep cut that split the butte and he kept Ebony moving at a canter. Once around the narrow point, he slowed to a walk, then stopped. He stepped down, motioned for Ezra to step down also, then handed the reins of Ebony to Cougar. "Keep going, find another cut to take cover in, just in case. But Ezra and I will go back to that cut and wait for them." He reached up to his saddle, patted Bobcat on the leg and said,

"You take care of Ebony for me son!" then slipped the saddle pistols from their holsters. He handed one to Ezra, nodded to Cougar as they started away, then looked at his friend.

"Did you see the cut back there?"

"Yup, figgered you would too."

"Then let's make for it and set up a welcome party for the Crow!"

Ezra chuckled, "I don't think they'll like our welcome!"

Gabe stationed himself on the shoulder of the butte on the right side of their trail, Ezra was below the trail and hidden in the brush. It was a little more than a half hour until they saw the three Crow warriors as they stopped to examine the trail. One man stepped down, looked at the tracks, touching the edges, then said something to the two others.

"They must know they are followed; they have started running," said Medicine Crow, pointing to the tracks, and with a swinging motion to the trail beside the river.

Yellowtail snorted, "We will get them!" and slapped legs to his mount. Medicine Crow was startled but swung aboard his horse and followed. Yellowtail set the pace, running his horse at a full gallop, lying low on his neck, the mane slapping him in the face. He looked up as he saw the butte that narrowed the passageway, then a quick glance showed the tracks of the white man and his woman were still digging deep and were running. He had a passing thought of an ambush, but quickly dismissed it, knowing their prey was probably frightened and fleeing. He slapped his legs to his mount, urging him on, and twisted around to see the others following close behind. As they neared the narrow point, Yellowtail slowed his mount to a canter and sat up to look as far ahead as possible, but seeing nothing alarming, looked back at the others and motioned them to keep up the pace.

Gabe saw the three riders mount up and kick their horses to a gallop and he gave the nighthawk cry to warn Ezra. The thunder of hooves increased, and he watched, lifting his rifle to take aim on the leader. As the leader slowed, Gabe squeezed the trigger and the Ferguson bucked as it spat smoke and lead. The lead rider sat up, leaned back and toppled from his galloping horse, falling and tumbling over into the sage. Gabe heard the bark of Ezra's rifle and saw the second rider slide to the side and fall to the ground, his horse never missing a step as he ran around the point, following the first horse.

The third rider lay low on his mount but believing the white man's gun was only good for one shot, he pointed his horse toward the first shooter, some-where on the shoulder of the butte. The horse leaned forward, digging hooves into the loose soil, nearing the position of the first shooter, and the rider was surprised to see the white man stand up, watching him urge his mount up the hillside.

Gabe watched the warrior charge up the hill, stood, withdrawing the big saddle pistol from his belt, cocking it as he brought it up. The rider was forcing his mount to climb the hillside, and Gabe shook his head. He called out in Shoshone, "You do not need to die today!"

But the man kept coming, screaming his war cry as he lifted his bow, arrow nocked. His horse was lunging, digging, and the man held tight with his legs, lifting his bow as he neared the white man. He screamed his war cry again, but before he could take aim, a cloud of grey smoke obscured the white man and Red Bird felt a blow to his chest that rocked him back. He grabbed at the mane of his horse, dropping his bow to the side as he fell forward on the horse's neck. He pulled on the rein to stop the horse climbing, slowly rose to look at the man that stood, a thin trail of smoke curling from his hand, and slipped to the side to fall on his back and roll down the slope a short distance. When Gabe came near, the man's eyes were staring sightlessly to the sky and he was dead.

Gabe reached into his possibles bag and began re-loading both the pistol and his Ferguson. He looked down and saw Ezra come from the brush to look at the other two Crow that lay near the trail, unmoving. When he finished reloading, he walked down the slope to join Ezra. He looked at his friend, "Well, I reckon that's that!"

"Yup. I think we oughta try to catch them horses, strip 'em and let 'em loose, ya reckon?"

"Yeah, I reckon."

17 / KUCCUNTIKKA

The women had not gone far and when they saw the men returning, they rode from the cut that marred the face of the mesa's slope. At Ezra's suggestion, the group opted to go to the grassy river-bank and rest for a spell, their horses well deserving of a break. Dove suggested, "I believe my husband is hungry so I will start a fire and make us a meal."

Gabe glanced to a smiling Ezra who had stretched out on the grass, his hat over his face until he heard Dove's suggestion. He jumped to his feet and happily went to fetching some firewood. The horses had been stripped of their gear and rubbed down and were enjoying their graze, the children, now wide awake, were chasing a pair of cottontails. Gabe sat leaning against the trunk of a standing dead gnarly cottonwood, watching the others and smiling at their antics. Cougar was busy with Dove as they prepared the morning meal. Gabe glanced to the clear sky, thinking *It's gonna be a pretty day!*

When they resumed their journey, Gabe led them to the flat-topped mesa, the lower of two stair stepped mesas that fell from the higher mountains. The trail was easier going than following the meandering river, and they lined out to the southeast, keeping the river in sight and off their left shoulder. The sun was warm upon their shoulders and the horses plodded on, kicking up a fine dust with every step. The riders repeatedly had to wipe the dry silt from their faces and shoulders, the children whimpering with every stop.

The sun was lowering over the Wind River range and sending lances of color overhead when they topped the end of a long ridge and dropped into a narrow valley, bottomed by a chuckling creek amidst willows and current bushes. With a nod, Gabe reined up and stepped down, lifted a very tired Bobcat from his saddle, accepted Fox from Cougar, and led the horses to the creek for water. Gabe sat the little ones down on the bank, let them put their feet in the cold water, then put his face in the water for a drink and a refreshing splash to rid his face and neck of the trail dust. He sat up, and with handfuls of water, washed the youngsters faces, gave them a drink, and sat back, enjoying the cool grass around them. Cougar had joined them and followed their actions, then suggested, "There's a deeper pool upstream there," nodding toward the mouth of a deep canyon that birthed the stream, "It would be good for all of us to bathe."

Gabe looked at Cougar, glanced at the little ones, and said, "Lead the way!"

Ezra saw them leaving and hollered, "Where you goin'?"

"Swimmin'!" shouted Gabe over his shoulder, as he bent to snatch up a pair of blankets from the bedrolls.

The water was cold, snowmelt that came from the high mountains, but it was refreshing, and the family wasted little time getting clean and getting out. As they dried off with the blankets, Cougar wrapped a blanket around her and trotted back to the packs to fetch fresh buckskins for the family and quickly returned. They had no sooner dressed than a call came from beyond the willows, "Hurry up! We wanna get in there too!" shouted Ezra.

While Ezra and family bathed, Gabe and family started the evening meal. Cougar put strips of smoked venison in the big pot together with onions, potatoes, and biscuit root, and soon had it simmering beside the fire. The skillet was reserved for corn pone. And the coffee pot was soon dancing on the rock. With everyone clean, fed, and tired, they soon turned in for the night, leaving guard duty to Wolf and the horses.

It was late afternoon the following day when they crested a small rise to see a wide expanse of green with a meandering river just below them. As they reined up to look around, to their right, the tall mountains stood like pillars holding up the blue sky, and the green valley invited them nearer. As they started to move, Gabe paused, held his hand to the side to stop the others, then reached to his saddle bags for the telescope. He stretched it out and lifted it to his eye, a slow grin painting his face as he lowered the scope, "I think its your people, Dove. They're butchering a bunch of buffalo the far end of this flat!"

Dove stood in her stirrups, shading her eyes and squinting, but the distance was too great. She glanced to Gabe and he handed the scope to Ezra to pass to Dove. She had not used it before, but Ezra showed her what to do and once it focused, she smiled and giggled, "Yes! Yes! It is!" She quickly handed the scope back to Ezra and nudged her mount forward, taking the lead as they left the rise. Gabe looked at Cougar, both smiling and laughing at Dove's antics, but quickly followed.

As they neared the killing field they saw each kill with several women busy at each one, braided rawhide ropes were used for the horses to pull the carcasses over to finish the skinning, camp dogs were bickering over gut piles, and carrion eaters had already started gathering. Overhead turkey buzzards, ravens, and eagles circled, picking a particular carcass or refuse pile to descend upon. Many of the men were busy dispatching wounded animals, while others helped with the butchering, but most paid little attention to the newcomers.

But they soon caused a stir when someone shouted, "Wolf! Wolf!" and several of the warriors grabbed for weapons until they saw the wolf walking among ridden horses that carried strangers, a white man and others. When Dove spotted a familiar face, she gigged her mount forward as she tossed the lead to the buckskin to Ezra. Around the nearest carcass, several women stood with bloodied hands, staring at the intruders, until recognition split the face of an older woman. Dove rode to the group quickly, slid to the ground before the buckskin slid to a stop, grabbed Squirrel from the saddle and turned to greet her mother, "Black Bear! I am your daughter, Grey Dove! And this is your granddaughter, Squirrel!"

The older woman broke from the group as she hustled toward Dove, arms outstretched and a broad smile showing below tear filled eyes. The women embraced, and Black Bear quickly took Squirrel from her mother, held her at arm's length and hugged her close. As she squeezed Squirrel tight, she looked at Dove and asked, "Where is your boy?"

Dove turned to see Ezra lowering Chipmunk to the ground and said, "Come here my son, this is your grandmother, Black Bear!" The boy timidly came to his mother, looking at Black Bear with shy eyes, but when the grandmother handed Squirrel back to her mother and bent down with arms wide toward Chipmunk, he smiled a bashful smile and walked into his grandmother's embrace.

Gabe and Cougar came alongside Ezra and Gabe looked at Ezra with a frown, "It sure doesn't look like they did too well on this hunt. I count only seven carcasses. That ain't enough to feed a village for very long."

"Yeah, I saw that too," replied Ezra, then nodded toward a small group of warriors that were coming near, "they might tell the story."

They recognized two of the men as Broken Lance, the leader of the village, and Chochoco, the war leader. As they came close, the stern looks and readied weapons changed to stoic expressions, but the weapons were held at the ready. Broken Lance spoke, "I see it is our friends, Black Buffalo and Spirit Bear. Do you come in peace?"

Gabe frowned, "We always come in peace, Broken Lance. Why would you think differently?"

"We have had much trouble in this season of greening and before. Our village has suffered, and we must be cautious."

"We have come to visit the family of my friend, the family of my woman that has crossed over, but we will leave if we are not wanted."

"Who is this?" asked Chochoco, motioning to Cougar Woman.

"This is my wife, *Doyadukubichi'*, Cougar Woman. She is a war leader of the Tukkutikka Shoshone," answered Gabe, as Cougar sat tall, scowling at the two leaders.

Chochoco stepped forward toward Cougar Woman and looked up, "I have heard of the war leader of the Tukkutikka, a brave leader and warrior. Welcome to our village."

Cougar relaxed her expression, nodded to Chochoco, "It is an honor to be among the people of my sister, Grey Dove."

Ezra had stepped to the ground and looked at Broken Lance and asked, "I see your warriors have taken buffalo, but this does not look like enough for the village. Was it a small herd?"

Broken Lance dropped his eyes to the ground and took a deep breath and looked at Black Buffalo, "We have few warriors to take the buffalo. Many are sick with the white man's spotted disease and unable to ride and hunt."

Ezra asked, "Have any died?"

"Yes, two have died, but more get sick. Our medicine man does not know what to do."

Ezra looked at Gabe, shaking his head, "How're you an' smallpox or measles?"

"I'm fine. Immune on both counts, and I know you had measles, but what about the pox?"

"I was exposed when some folks in our church had

a spell of it, so I think I'm alright."

Gabe glanced to Cougar, then to Dove, "But they aren't!"

"No, but they both can gather some herbs and such, depending on what it is."

"Yeah, I reckon," responded Gabe, somewhat resolutely, then looked at Broken Lance, "Let us help your shaman, we've seen this disease and it could kill many if we can't stop it."

Broken Lance stepped back as if he had been struck, then frowned, "Why would you do this?"

"Your people are our people. They need help. But you need to keep everyone away from the village, no one in or out. Is there anyone that has been sick and alright now?"

The chief frowned, looked at Chochoco and back at Gabe, "Yes, *Weahwewa,* Wolf Dog, and Crazy Fox."

Chochoco spoke up, "The woman, Laughing Turtle."

"If you could get them to come with us and help, we will start for the village. Are you above the falls?"

"Yes, our summer encampment," answered Broken Lance, pointing to the cut between the foothills that sided the Wind River Range.

"Your people can return, but not into the village. They could camp near our cabin or above it, but no closer," directed Gabe.

As they rode into the deep cut, Gabe and Ezra

explained to the women what would be necessary, "You'll be able to stay in the cabin, keep the horses near or into the upper pasture, Dove knows where that is, and we will need you to gather all the aspen buds, bear grass, and any thing else that will be good for temperatures, and such. The sick ones will have a rash, so something soothing for their skin would be good, sore throats that need a soothing tea, and some will have diarrhea and vomiting, so whatever helps that. But remember, you cannot come close or you'll get it too and we don't want the younguns' comin' down with it."

Dove offered, "We will fix your meals, and bring them close for you."

Ezra said, "That's what I like to hear."

The men looked at one another, knowing what they were in for, but it was necessary to do what they could to help the people. Gabe said, "According to what Broken Lance described, I think it's measles. That's bad enough."

"Yeah, I just hope it ain't smallpox!" declared Ezra, both men speaking on the down low to keep the women from becoming even more concerned. But it would be a battle and not the kind of fighting they were accustomed to entering.

18 / RIO GRANDE

It was four days of travel following the Camino Real, but the trail seemed to fade, and the men of the Spanish expedition chose to keep near the river. The chosen route rode the high flats that overlooked the arroyo that carried the ancient waterway known as the Rio Grande. The land was littered with sage and greasewood, interspersed with clusters of rabbit brush and buffalo grass, while all about them they picked their trail through cacti. Coyotes, jackrabbits, armadillos, roadrunners, and rattlesnakes were plentiful. To the east, timbered foothills shouldered mountain peaks of a long range that marched north and south, some of the peaks still holding to patches of snow and glacier ice. In the flats, random timbered hills and buttes seemed to rise from nothing to lift their heads into the empty sky. The sun hung high above in a clear blue sky, horses and mules and men hung their heads in the stifling heat.

"What's that?" queried Diego, pointing across the wide arroyo that carried the Rio Bravo del Norte, or the Rio Grande. A dust cloud trailed two riders bouncing on the rumps of a pair of burros, as they angled their mounts toward the high mountains, another pair of loaded burros following after, and they sided a smaller river that came from the mountains.

The Capitan reined up, frowning as he shaded his eyes to look, reached into his saddle bags for the telescope and lifted it to his eye for a better look. They had just crossed a deep arroyo that fed run-off to the larger river and now were atop the flat above the gorge. He scanned the flatlands on the far side of the river, saw the riders and frowned. "I cannot tell if they are natives or Mexicans. They are riding and leading burros!" he declared, still watching the riders as they distanced themselves from the riverbed. He lowered the scope, looking at the terrain, pointing to the north, "We should cross this gorge and take the other side. The smaller river spreads out there, and the land is green on the far side. We would do well to cross over, not so many arroyos to slow us down." He lifted the scope again, moving it to view the riverbed and the grassy flats on the far side, then nodded his head, "There, where the rivers merge, the walls are easier, and it looks like there is a trail into the bottom." He paused as he scoped more of the bottom, "That slope drops into the river!" he declared, pointing to a point of land that pushed into the river bottom. It was a gradual slope and would be easily ridden, and the river in the bottom appeared to widen and offer an easy crossing.

Diego swung his arm high, motioning to the others to follow and pointed his mount to the far mesa with the sloping end pointed out by the Capitan. Within the hour, they were in the bottom of the wide arroyo and across the river and moving easily along the trail that led to the confluence of rivers. The smaller stream cascaded down the steep slope, showing nothing but whitewater as the snow melt chuckled its way to the bottom.

"Capitan, that trail leads to the top!" said Diego, pointing to the oft-used trail that sided the small stream. As they entered the smaller gorge, the trail narrowed and climbed the basaltic slope on the south wall of the narrow gorge.

Capitan de Almeida nodded to Diego, "You take the lead," motioning the man ahead. Diego looked back at the Capitan, twisted in his saddle to look at the narrow trail and took a deep breath, nudging his mount forward. The narrow trail started up the steep black slope, every step of the horse seeming to cause rocks to tumble to the bottom as a reminder of the danger of this eyebrow trail. When he was twenty feet away, the Capitan motioned the next in line to follow, sending the men in the long line to wind like a black snake up the narrow and uncertain trail. When the last man, leading the last mule, passed the Capitan, he took a deep breath and nudged his mount forward.

As Diego neared the crest of the trail, he leaned out to look below and guessed the river to be over two hundred fifty feet below, appearing like a white thread lying at the bottom of the basaltic slope. A shoulder of the mesa pushed into the trail and Diego's mount balked, not liking the looks of the narrow trail that hung over the gorge. Diego slipped to the ground and walked to the point, craning around to ensure the trail continued, then walked back to his horse, picked up the reins and chose to lead the animal around the bump out. He moved easily on the trail, always hugging the wall, and refusing to look over the edge, the rein clutched tightly in his hand, and glanced back to see the horse leaning into the wall, the inside stirrup pushing back to his flank. The black gelding followed close behind Diego and the pair was soon around the point. Diego mounted up and called out to the rider following, "It is best if you lead your horse around the point! The trail is narrow, but good."

The second rider, Vasco de Gama, led his mount around the abutment, carefully picking each step as he glanced over the edge, wide-eyed. The pack mule lead was tied to the saddle horn but stretched out tight as the mule followed around the point. Vasco untied the lead of the mule from the horn, stuck his foot in the stirrup and swung aboard. His sudden move startled the mule who pulled back on the lead, jerking Vasco's arm behind him, but the strong arm pulled the lead tight as he leaned forward and gigged his mount. They had gone but a few steps when the big dapple-grey mount spooked, jerking his head high and rearing up, pawing at the air. Vasco heard the unmistakable rattle of a diamond back, saw at a glance the coiled snake on a narrow ledge, as he fought for control of the horse. But the big grey was frightened, back stepped, and lost his footing. The weight of his rider and the uncertain footing startled the animal even more, as he swung his head side to side, jerking at the taut reins and feeling the blunt spurs in his ribs. The horse screamed a whinny, backstepped again, and his hind hooves dropped from the shelf. Vasco kicked his feet free from the stirrups, leaned well over the horse's neck, but it was too late. The screams of horse and rider echoed across the narrow canyon as they tumbled end over end, feet and arms flailing in the emptiness, to crash against the rocks at stream side. The distant echo of the screams falling silent as frozen men stared at the bottom.

It was just over an hour after they started up the trail that the last of the riders crested the mesa, followed closely by the Capitan. After killing the snake, Diego had led de Gama's mule to the top and everyone had stepped to the ground and were standing beside their mounts and pack mules, stretching their legs, and talking. The Capitan also stepped down, looked from Diego to the men and asked, "Why have we stopped?"

"To rest the animals, mi Capitan. The trail made many of them skittish and they need to rest but a short while."

The next week saw the Capitan as a hard taskmaster, driving the expedition north without stopping for rest except at night. Although they resupplied at Alburquerque, they could have stopped at Taos for a time of rest, or more supplies, but they passed by the last outpost of civilization with nothing but a glance at the fortified compound. Now, several days after passing Taos, around the camp the grumbling of the men was constant, most complaining about the relentless sun, dust, and constant moving. When one of the men, Alvar Cabeza de Vaca approached Diego, he asked, "When will we get a day of rest? We are exhausted and the animals are stumbling!"

"I know, I know. I have asked, but he ignores me. He gets that wild look in his eyes and snarls like a crazed cougar. He beats his horse and threatens to have me whipped!"

Alvar looked at Diego, wide-eyed, surprised at the man. The men of the expedition willingly followed

Diego, but the Capitan was unmerciful, and many had talked about abandoning the expedition, but in a strange land they had nowhere to go and the Capitan had threatened to have them shot. Alvar glanced around, looking for the Capitan, then whispered, "What if we . . . you know, what if we . . ." then made the motion of slitting his throat.

Diego shook his head, "No, no. We cannot do that." He looked past the fire to where the Capitan had spread his blankets, saw the man fidgeting with his weapons, and continued. "We must wait until we find the gold. He has the map, but it's what he knows that is not on the map that is important." He nodded to the long line of jagged peaks, "Those are the Sangre de Cristo mountains, we are near the beginning of them. There we cross into another long valley that follows the Sawatch range, according to his map, and after that we will be near the place of the gold." He paused, looking at the others that sat by the fire, "We will talk again, soon."

19 / STRUGGLE

They put their horses in the stable by the cabin, helped the women put things in the cabin, and Gabe said, "Now, we'll go to the camp, and if the two of you can do what you can to gather any of the plants we need to help, something for a rash," he rubbed his arm as he spoke, "and for a fever, maybe something for a tea, and something for vomiting and diarrhea. Leave it by the creek, but don't cross over, and we'll meet you there."

"I know many things that will help. We will gather them and prepare them for you," answered Cougar, glancing to Dove as she nodded her head, agreeing.

"Good, we can't do this without you. We'll probably get some others to gather things as well, but you know better what will work, so we'll depend on you," stated Gabe.

They embraced the women and walked down

to the encampment. When they entered the camp, Gabe and Ezra were welcomed by two women that stopped them to tell about the sickness. The first woman said, "You must not come near! There is much sickness here!"

"We know grandmother," using the term of respect for the white-haired woman, "that is why we are here. Do you have the sickness?" asked Gabe.

"No, no, not yet, but others do!" she declared, frowning at the man she recognized as a friend of the people.

"Are there others like you, helpers, I mean, that do not have the sickness?"

"Yes, there are three other women that are tending the sick."

"Would you please bring them here, we must talk. But before you do, tell me, how many are sick?"

"Three hands, maybe more."

"Tell me about the sickness," continued Gabe, "we are here to help."

The woman known as Night Star, explained that some were very warm, some had tiny spots and bumps, some were sick at their stomachs causing them to vomit and have diarrhea. Gabe asked, "Tiny spots, bumps? Not open sores?"

She nodded her head as she rubbed her arm, "Many little bumps here, and here," putting her hand to her face and neck. "Some are covered here," putting her hand to her chest and stomach.

Gabe nodded, "Bring the others, please."

As the women waddled off, Gabe turned to Ezra, "Sounds more like measles than Small Pox. I hope she's right."

When the old woman returned with three other women, and the shaman, Walks in the Clouds, they stood before Gabe and Ezra showing skeptical and stern expressions. Gabe began, "We know this sickness and we will help those that are sick. Have any of you had this same sickness?"

One of the women, Dancing Bird, spoke up, "I have had this sickness. I was not as sick as these are, but I had the bumps and was also very warm."

Gabe stepped forward and asked to see her arms, looked at her neck and face, and nodded. "You can stay and help, but the rest of you and any others in the camp that are not sick, must leave immediately. But do not go near any others, you must stay by yourselves. Take your blankets, food, whatever you need, but stay away from the camp for this many," holding up two hands, all fingers extended, "days. If you get sick, return here to let us help you." He looked at Dancing Bird and Night Star, "We will need lot of Bear root, some willows, and any of the red buds from the aspen. If you know of anything that will make a tea to help with the fever, that will be needed too." The women nodded, and quickly moved away, glancing back at the men as they started to the lodges to check on the ill. The shaman stayed, looking at Gabe, then stated, "I will stay and help my people!"

"Good, good. But if you get sick, you must stay away from the others. Understood?"

"Yes. But why do you not get sick?"

Gabe grinned, "We," motioning to Ezra, "had this sickness long ago, and once you've had it and lived, you will no longer get this sickness."

The shaman slowly nodded, frowning at the men, but accepted what was said.

For two weeks, the three men, Gabe, Ezra and the shaman, worked tirelessly with their helpers, administering balms and ointments, teas, and powders, to bring down the temperatures, soothe the rashes, and comfort the sick. Gabe did not know what all was used, trusting Cougar and Dove and the other women to make the balms. He knew one of the most common was from the root of the Osha, or bear root. But goldenrod, arrowleaf, beebalm, sage and the buds of aspen and the inner bark of willows, were commonly used for their needs. As patients recovered, they would be put to work tending the others, and by the end of the two weeks, they had lost only one, a young man that had been stricken early, fought hard, but lost his battle when the pneumonia took his breath and life.

Dove's parents, Red Pipe and Black Bear, stayed

in the cabin with Dove and the children, enjoying the private time together immensely. Although they missed their daughter and Dove's sister, Otter, they readily accepted Cougar Woman as Spirit Bear's new wife, and treated her and the little ones, like their own.

By the end of two weeks and with all the patients recovered, the chief, Broken Lance, declared a feast and celebration was due, and sent the women to their lodges and cookfires to prepare. It was a welcome respite, and everyone gladly went to work to prepare for the gathering, feasting, and dancing. Gabe and Ezra returned to their cabin for the first time since they returned to the Popo Agie valley. They were met at the door by their women, who embraced them, then with a bit of a mischievous smile on their faces, led them away from the cabin and upstream of the encampment.

As they came to a cluster of trees and a grassy knoll that sided the creek, Gabe and Ezra spotted a small domed structure with smoke coming from the peak. The men immediately recognized it as a sweat lodge and the women nodded, "There are clean buckskins there beside the stream and blankets for drying. We have already used the lodge, now it is yours."

The men looked at their wives, grinning, knowing that after their time of tending to others and the long days and nights, a spell in the sweat lodge and a fresh dip in the creek would do wonders for them. Ezra looked at Gabe, then to Dove, "This will be great," he said as he embraced his woman. Gabe did much the same and the two men were soon stripping off their clothes and ducking into the lodge.

It was a relaxing time to sit in the hot lodge, steam rising as they splashed water on the hot coals and rocks, the deep cleansing that came from an extended time in the lodge was just what the men needed to rid themselves of the stink of the sickness and all that had accompanied the time with the ill. Once cleansed, they ducked out and dove into the deep backwater pool, only to be shocked at the icy waters, but the cold water was refreshing and revitalizing. They climbed from the water to dry off and don the fresh clothes, to return to the cabin.

It was a welcome sight to see the first cabin they built on their wilderness journey. It was tucked under the overhang of the huge monolith that stood on the shoulder of the taller mountains. Wide enough for a spacious cabin and a stable for the horses on the cold winter nights, it had been their first home with their new wives, Grey Dove and Pale Otter. It was also where Wolf joined them, after they found him in the deep cavern behind the cabin, apparently having wandered away from his mother's side and ended up in the cavern and eventually the cabin. There were many memories that returned when they entered the warm abode, but the presence of Dove's parents, the children, and their loving wives, were all the men needed or wanted.

It was three days after the night of the feast, that the two families were mounted and leaving the village behind. Dove twisted in her saddle to look back at her mother, waving as they left. It had been a good visit, and they would return, but the unknown wilderness beckoned the two men with wanderlust in their blood, and they were bound to the south, to explore and discover the new lands of the Rocky Mountains.

They rode into the rising sun, dropping from the high country and taking the trail that sided the Popo Agie creek through the canyon. They passed the point where the creek disappeared into the face of a cliff and rose from deep underground about a hundred yards further down the canyon. When they broke from the canyon, the broad vista of the green valley seemed to welcome them with open arms. Ezra was in the lead and turned south, knowing they would continue southward for many days. On their initial journey to the far blue mountains they came almost due west from a smaller range that bordered the flats with the North Platte river, the river they followed from the east. But now they were bound for high mountains to the south, some said the mountains there were even taller than those they had already explored, but the distant wilderness beckoned, and they were following.

20 / ROCKIES

Although the land looked flat and barren, it was lush with the vegetation of the great plains. Sage, greasewood, rabbit brush and bunch grass was prominent, but clusters of prickly pear, cholla, and many other cacti showed early summer blossoms to add color to what showed as dreary colors of pale yellow, dim brown, and faded green. Far to the south, the faint line of jagged peaks beckoned them onward.

At first glance the country looked barren, dry, and uninhabitable, yet it was dotted with tanks, ponds, and small lakes, most shallow, many stagnant, but ample water for the thirsty traveler. They let the horses have their heads, Wolf in the lead, and without fail, they moved from water to water in the overland trek. Days stretched into a week before they neared the mountains. Two ranges, the Medicine Bow, and the Sierra Madre, stood before them, with a wide valley between and it was that valley that offered rest and refuge. They came to the upper reaches of the North Platte River, although they did not know it as such, and followed it upstream into the fertile green valley of the headwaters.

The river was lined with tall cottonwoods, green leaves rattling in the breeze, aspen with their silvery green leaves quaking, thick willows, and many different berry bushes. Deep green grass carpeted the banks and the grey/green sage stood off a ways with the bunch grass and more. The foothills were thick with juniper, cedar, and a few ponderosa, at least where the rocky escarpments allowed green to show, and bald slopes were spotted with elk. Big horn sheep gathered near the river's edge, timidly watching the intruders as they rode beside the deep waters. The river had cut a deep channel between the foothills, pushing them aside for the constant flow of snow melt to escape the highlands.

It was beautiful country, cool crisp air that prompted the riders to breathe deep after so many days of spitting dust, and the sun was cradled in the high mountains off their right shoulder, giving warning of the arrival of dusk and its big sister, darkness. The river forked and Ezra bore to the west, southwest, following the meandering stream.

The foothills soon gave way to a wide-open valley that appeared to lay between a wide barren ridge to the east, some nearby buttes on the west, and taller mountains further west. Ezra chose a spot near the river, tall cottonwoods offering good shelter, and a stream that summoned the fisherman. It was in the dim light of dusk when they made camp on the grassy bank, clusters of willows shading the waters, and cottonwoods and alders that gave shelter.

"This would be a good place to rest up a few days, ya reckon?" asked Ezra as he slipped the saddle from the bay, glancing over to Gabe.

"Suits me!" answered Gabe, finishing stripping the packs from the horses and mule. They led the animals to water, rubbing them down as they drank, and Ezra said, "Lookee there," pointing to the rippling water, "There's so many fish in there, they're just beggin' me to come get 'em!"

"Then get to it!" declared Gabe, "I'll finish with the horses."

Ezra did not have to be offered the chance twice, he quickly went to the packs to fetch his fishing tackle and moved upstream from the horses and set about his favorite pastime, or at least one of them. When Gabe finished with the horses, he picketed them separately and far enough apart so each would have ample graze, and when finished, he joined the women and the children near the cookfire. He had no sooner taken a seat than Ezra came back to the camp in a bit of a hurry with an expression that told of trouble. Gabe jumped to his feet, as Ezra said, "Company! Looks to be about six or eight, prob'ly Ute. Ain't this Ute country?"

"That's what Broken Lance said. He'd traveled this way before, said the Ute were not friends with the Shoshone, but weren't as bad as the Blackfoot."

"Oh, that's encouraging!" declared Ezra as both he and Gabe fetched their rifles. Cougar and Dove had heard, and both had their rifles ready and nearby, but they would stay with the children. Ezra led the way as the two men worked their way back on the trail, staying close to the willows. Within moments they saw the riders coming, and Gabe stepped to the middle of the trail, rifle held muzzle down, but cocked and ready. Ezra stood at his side, positioned in a similar manner, his war club showing over his shoulder.

The warriors had been looking down at the tracks and were surprised when they looked up to see the two men standing before them. With less than twenty yards between them, Gabe spoke, "Ya'eh teh!" It was a common greeting, similar in many languages, and understood by most. Broken Lance had said the languages of the Ute and the Shoshone were similar, but nothing was certain.

The party had reined up, spreading out to either side of the two warriors in the front, and Gabe counted eight. The man in front, obviously their

leader, had a hair-pipe breastplate, long braids tuft-
ed with dyed rabbit fur, two notched feathers stood
erect from a topknot at the back of his head, and
fringed buckskins covered his legs. His neck was
decorated with a multi-layered bone necklace, and
a silver band was prominent on his upper bicep. He
had a Spanish musket laying across the withers of
his mount, while the others appeared to be armed
only with bows. With none holding lances, Gabe
thought this was a hunting party. With no response
from the warriors, Gabe sat his rifle butt on his toe,
holding the weapon close with his arm, so he could
use both hands to sign as he spoke. "We are visitors
from the land far to the east. We have our families
with us and welcome you to our fire." He spoke in
the language of the Shoshone and watched their
expressions for understanding.

The leader looked at those on either side, slow-
ly nodding, then answered, "This is the land of the
Yapudttka Ute, and I am the war chief, White Raven.
Why are you here?"

Before Gabe could answer, Wolf pushed his way
between the men, head lowered, lip snarling, hackles
raised, and mouth open. Gabe casually reached down
to touch Wolf's scruff, spoke softly to him, "Easy boy,
easy." He had not taken his eyes from the leader, but
let his hand drop to the trigger guard of his rifle.

The warriors had shown alarm when Wolf came

between the men, for he was an uncommonly large beast and his manner showed anything but friendliness. The leader had unconsciously drawn back, eyes wide, and watched as the men stood firm before them, with the white man's hand on the neck of the Wolf.

Gabe answered, "We are just passing through. We came to see this great land and meet the people of this land," he paused, then added, "I am Spirit Bear, and this is Black Buffalo." The leader was staring at the wolf but lifted his eyes as Gabe spoke. Gabe had understood when the one known as White Raven spoke, but he used sign so the others would understand.

White Raven motioned to one of his men, and the man came forward, slid the carcass of a big horn sheep off the rump of his horse, letting it fall to the ground almost at the feet of Gabe. White Raven said, "We will make camp, there," pointing with his chin to the grass near the stream, "and will come to your camp soon. That will be meat for all."

Ezra handed his rifle to Gabe, snatched up the sheep and draped it over his shoulders and started to camp. Gabe watched the Ute move from the trail, then turned to follow Ezra. When they returned to camp, Ezra said, "We're gonna have comp'ny for dinner, so here's some meat!"

Dove looked at him, and with hands on her hips, said, "Then get to cuttin' it!"

Ezra was a little taken aback, but grinned and said,

"Yes m'am!" and dropped the carcass next to a broad flat rock they had used for a prep table and went to work. Gabe cut several willow withes, then dropped them next to the fire and joined Ezra in the task of cutting meat. In a short while, the fire had been made larger, and many sticks with strips of steak hung over the flames. The women had made additional corn dodgers and put the remaining potatoes and more in the big pot that was bubbling at the fireside.

White Raven led the warriors into the camp, Gabe noticing they came without their bows, but each man had the typical knife and tomahawk at their belts. They sat together near the lower end of the fire, but all were looking at the women and the children as they waited. Gabe started introducing everyone, "This is my wife, Cougar Woman, she is a war leader of the Tukkutikka Shoshone, and these," pointing to his boys, "are my sons, Bobcat and Fox." He nodded to Ezra who spoke up, "And this," he stepped close and put his arm around Dove's waist, "is my wife, Grey Dove, of the Kuccuntikka Shoshone, and my children, my son Chipmunk, and my daughter, Squirrel."

"You have fine families," stated White Raven. "I too have a woman and sons."

Gabe had noticed White Raven looking at the horses, and grinned when he asked, "Is that black a stallion?"

"Yes, and a very good one, too."

"I have a mare that needs breeding, will you be here long?"

"Just a couple days, but if you want to bring your mare, I'm sure Ebony wouldn't mind."

Gabe stood, and motioned to White Raven, "Come take a look." Gabe knew that their horses would be the envy of just about anyone, for they were all well chosen and bred, from the steeldust mustang to Gabe's big Andalusian stallion. But he also knew they were visitors in the land of a people they did not know and would have to be watchful of those that might think they could easily take the horses, a tempting prize for anyone. As they neared the animals, Gabe spoke softly to Ebony, and put his hand on the horse's rump, letting him know he was near. The two men walked alongside, White Raven reaching out to touch the well-muscled mount, smiling as he saw the slight arch to the stallion's neck, the broad chest, and the rippling shoulders.

"He is a fine animal, is he good as a stallion?"

Gabe grinned, motioned him to follow and went near the appaloosa and her colt. The long-legged yearling boldly walked to Gabe, nose outstretched for his touch, and let Gabe run his hands over his neck and back, enjoying the attention. Gabe grinned at White Raven, "This is one of his colts."

The Ute war chief grinned, "It is a fine colt." His expression changed as he thought, then looked at

Gabe, "What would it take for you to put your stallion with my mare?"

Gabe chuckled, "Just bring your mare here, and let us be friends."

The war chief slowly grinned, "It will be done," as he nodded, then stroked the back of the spotted colt.

21 / HEADWATERS

The expedition rounded the north end of the Sangre de Cristo mountain range when they took the cut between the north end of the Sangres and the south end of the Sawatch range. The trail dropped them into a wide, fertile valley with the long range of Sawatch mountains marching off to the north, and rugged foothills paralleled on the east edge of the green valley. That was four days ago, and after bypassing a deep and perilous canyon that gave the river a straight south riverway, they sided the river marked as the Arkansa on the ancient maps of the Capitan.

As they neared the end of the fourth day following the river, they broke into a wider valley that prompted them to stop and take in the view. "Those mountains! So high, and with snow still on them and their heads are in the clouds!" declared Diego, staring in awe at the massive granite tipped peaks on the west edge of the flat-bottomed valley. "And that one, it is the biggest one we have seen!" he stated as he stood in his stirrups and pointed.

A big herd of elk was lazily grazing in the deep grass, the herd bull with velvet covered antlers lifted his head to look at the visitors to his domain. When no one moved, he casually pushed closer to the herd, but most paid little attention to him. This was the time of year that bulls were seldom with the cows as they nursed the new calves. It was more common to see bunches of bulls, young and old, gathered together but apart and even distant from the cows, but this bull stayed near the herd, protective of the gangly calves, while watching over the cows.

The Capitan sat his mount beside Diego, dug the map from his saddle bags and stretched it out, laying it on the pommel of his saddle, an action his mount had become accustomed to and knew he had time to snatch some grass to munch. Francisco traced the line of the river, to the upper edge, saw the notations and glanced up at Diego. "This is the valley. This is where the Brigadier and others believe is Quivera, the Seven Cities of Cibola. But they believe there were no cities, no, they believe it is the seven forks of the river that hold the gold!" He looked again at the map, stood in his stirrups, and pointed, "The first is there," pointing across the river to a notch in the foothills that carried a feeder creek that splashed into the river. "Another is there," pointing further upstream, "Another comes from there," pointing across the valley to the timber covered foothills that lay like a dark blue skirt of the mountains, "and the others are further upstream." He nodded his head as he sat back in the seat of his saddle, a complacent expression on his face that turned into a grin as he looked at his subordinate.

"We will go further and make camp in a central location to all the tributaries, then we will disperse bands to each of the streams to find the gold!" He looked back at the men, summoned the sergeants near, "Sergeant Alvares," and standing in his stirrups and pointing, "After we camp, and you are properly instructed, you and your men will take that stream there, coming from the hills."

The Sergeant stood to look, nodding as he turned to face the Capitan, "Si, mi Capitan."

"Sergeant Corte-Real," began the Capitan, twisting in his saddle and pointing to another stream that shouldered a long flat-topped finger ridge, "that will be your assignment."

He looked to the others, "Let us go further," he stated as he nudged his mount to a trot. The others followed close behind, but after about a mile, he dropped into a walk and the horses blew, snatching up mouthfuls of grass as they moved. A little over another mile, they came to a sizable stream that came from the mountains and the Capitan pushed his mount into the crystalline shallow water, to lead the crossing over of a gravel bar as they watched the trout scatter upstream. As they mounted the far bank, the Capitan looked at Sergeant de Noli, "You and your men will take this stream."

The Sergeant nodded, "Si, mi Capitan."

They stayed on the east side of the Arkansa, now a much smaller stream as they neared the headwaters, and the Capitan reined up as something caught his eye at the edge of the thick black timber that had pushed nearer the river. He pulled out his scope and lifted it for a look, shook his head and handed the scope to Diego. After a quick look, Diego lowered the scope and looked to the Capitan. "That's a good-sized village."

"Yes, and they are about five or six miles back in the trees, but that is good, unless they attack us."

"Good?" asked Diego, frowning.

"Yes. If we find the gold, we will need help getting it and slave labor is the cheapest labor," he stated, emphatically, and gigged his mount forward.

Diego scowled, glanced back at the men, "Keep your rifles ready!" he ordered, then followed the Capitan.

The Capitan paused, looked across the river to a smaller stream that came from a massive alluvial plain that lay in the lap of a long range of jagged mountains, and pushed well into the valley. He grinned, "I will take that stream," he declared and pushed on a little further, moving closer to the river. He stood in his stirrups, pointed across the river to the timber topped mesa, "There, where the trees come from the mesa, we will camp there!"

They followed the Capitan as he pushed through the willows and alders, then into the cold shallow waters of the Arkansa. Within moments, they were out of the willows and moving to the trees. As Diego looked around, he was pleased to see the Capitan had chosen an excellent site for their camp. The tall ponderosa offered good shelter, the grass was deep and plentiful for the animals, and the water was near. He knew they might be here for quite some time and was glad it offered all they would need.

When they moved into the trees, the Capitan told Diego, "Further upstream," nodding to the north, you should find two more forks. You will take one and Sergeant Fernandes will take the other."

"I see, mi Capitan, but what is it we are to do?"

"Find gold, of course! But I will show you and the others just how to do that before you go, and we will go tomorrow."

After their early morning meal, the men walked the short distance to the river below their camp. The river snaked through the valley bottom, splitting several times to leave wide islands between the divided streams. Where they approached, there lay a long gravel bar that gently sloped to the rippling stream. The Capitan stood at water's edge, lifted the round almost flat pan overhead and began, "You will be panning the stream for any sign of gold. Now this is how it's done," and dropped to one knee at water's edge, reached into the water and scooped a pan full of mud, silt, and gravel, then as he began to slosh it side to side, "Gold is heavy, even the little flakes, and as you gently wash the water side to side, the mud and rocks, most of them anyway, will be splashed out, and any gold will remain." He demonstrated the move, slowly moving the pan in a circular motion, washing the lighter soil and rocks out of the pan, "Now, you may have to remove the rocks," and demonstrated picking up and examining each of the stones, "but look for any sign of gold in each one, for gold is often found in quartz, the white crystal type rock," but not seeing any, he discarded each of the rocks, and began to move the pan again. When the mud and silt were gone, the water was clear, and in the bottom of the pan were three tiny flecks of gold. The Capitan smiled, and nodded as he held out the pan, "Like this, see?"

The men stepped forward, eyes wide and looked at the tiny flecks in the bottom of the pan, then stepped back and chattered among themselves until one man asked, "But there's so little, it would take forever to get even a hand full!"

"This is very little, and not of great interest. That is why we will try the streams that lead into the river. If any of you have a pan with eight or more flecks, then mark that place and work your way upstream to see if there will be more. At the end of each day, we will return to camp and share what we have learned. Our patrons believe there is much gold in this land, but it is up to us to find it!"

"And when we find a place where there is much gold, then what?" asked another worker.

"Then we will all work that area, finding where it comes from and if necessary, mine it!"

"So, we will not be wading in the water all the time?"

"No, no. We need much more than a few flakes that can be taken in a pan," explained Francisco. "Now, each sergeant will take three men and a mule, and two men will stay in camp to watch over the horses and gear. There is an Indian village beyond those trees," pointing to the trees beyond the river, "and you must always be watchful. We do not know if they are friendly or not, so, always have one man to watch, and have your rifles ready."

The men mumbled and grumbled as they walked back to camp, uneasy with the thought of the nearby village, but the greed for gold was overwhelming. The men were quickly chosen by the sergeants, Diego and Francisco, and they rode away from the camp. Diego and Sergeant Fernandes and their men riding upstream of the Arkansa, to their dividing point. At the confluence with another sizable stream from the east, Diego parted ways with Fernandes and his men, moving upstream of the smaller fork.

The Capitan was smiling as he led his band of three back to the creek that flowed from the alluvial plain, believing he had chosen the better of the tributaries for himself. With his knowledge of geology gained from his studies at university in Spain, he believed this plain would show the most color, for the entirety of the alluvial fan had come from the higher mountains where quartz and limestone were abundant.

Each of the groups were anxious on their first day of panning for gold, gone were the many days of dry, hot, dusty travel, for they had arrived at their destination, and this was where they would soon realize their dreams of wealth and plenty. Each sergeant assigned two men to begin panning, while one man stood guard, and the sergeant moved further upstream to scout out the stream and possibilities. When Diego and Duarte Fernandes parted company, the sergeant wasted little time before going to the water. He chose to go to the water first, anxious to see gold in the pan, but he was disappointed. After several tries, carefully washing the excess from the pan, he was disappointed and took his group further upstream.

Diego had been just as anxious as the others, but he allowed his men to take to the water first. The first man was unsuccessful, but the second man showed color. When the third man dipped his pan in the backwater behind a big boulder, he carefully washed the mud and rocks from the pan, then froze in place as he stared at the bottom of the pan. A slow smile split his face as he began to tremble, "Look! Look!" he shouted, pointing to the bottom of the pan. The other men splashed into the water and stared at the bottom of the pan, where at least eight flakes slowly moved in the wash of the water held in nervous hands. But the most exciting was a small nugget, no bigger than the smallest of fingernails on the man's hand, glistening in the clear water and bright sunshine. He slowly reached for the little nugget, grasping it between his thumb and forefinger and lifted it closer to his face to examine the shiny stone. "Gold," he whispered, then a little louder, "Gold!" and louder still, "GOLD!" He turned to face Diego, and started splashing about in the water, until Diego held out his hand, and said, "Put it in my hand, and pan for more!" he looked at the other men, "You too!" he declared, as he accepted the tiny flakes and little nugget from the man known as João Grego. Diego went to his horse and retrieved his pan to begin panning with the others.

The men worked tirelessly throughout the day, but by the end of the day they realized they had exhausted the little pocket of gold they found below the boulder, but they had learned a little about the nature of gold, and they would be the better for it as they planned to continue further upstream. When they returned to camp and each of the leaders compared their findings, Diego's groups had done more than any other, although several had found sign. When he laid out the small nugget, and another slightly larger, then the small pile of flakes, the men gathered close and looked carefully as the nuggets were passed around for everyone to see.

And as the excited men clamored together, thrilled about the find, they did not see the five natives move away through the trees to return to their horses and go tell their chief what they had seen among the camp of the Spanish invaders.

22 / SOUTHWARD

And the Ute war leader, White Raven, did return. With a wide grin, he led the high-stepping paint mare into the camp of Gabe and company. Their horses were tethered in the tall grass and when White Raven led the mare near, Ebony was the first to turn, head high, as he watched the visitors come near the camp. He nickered at the mare, who stepped sideways, straining at her lead, to look at the horses on the grassy flat. She lifted her head and nickered back at the big black who tossed his head and pranced about.

Gabe laughed as he watched the antics of his big black Andalusian stallion, then lifted a hand high to greet White Raven. Beside the man, aboard a paint with similar markings to the mare, a woman sat erect, and stoic as she looked about the camp. Cougar and Dove looked at the woman, then stepped close. Dove spoke first, "I am Grey Dove, and my friend is Cougar Woman. Step down and come to the fire and visit with us."

The woman looked down at the two Shoshone women who greeted her, glancing from one to the other, then to White Raven who nodded. She swung her leg over the rump of her horse and stepped to the ground, turning as she said, "I am the wife of White Raven, war leader of the Ute people. I am called Yellow Bird, like the bird with the long song."

As the women spoke with one another and began to move away, White Raven stepped from his mount, keeping the lead taut on the mare, and turned to look at Gabe. The mare had captured Gabe's attention with its unusual color. With the bold color of a palomino, and the white markings of a paint, the mare tossed her head with the long flowing mane of both colors. She struggled to look at Ebony and Ebony was straining at his tether to come near. Gabe chuckled, "Looks like she's caught the eye of my stallion, reckon we better get them together?"

"Yes, she is anxious," answered White Raven, turning toward the horses in the grassy flat.

Gabe paused, looked around, then pointed to a break in the trees, "You take her through there, it's a little meadow with plenty of grass, and tie her fast to a tree but with a long lead. Then I'll bring him to her, and they can work things out themselves."

White Raven grinned, nodded, and started to the

little meadow. Within moments, Gabe brought Ebony prancing into the grassy nook, slipped the halter from his head, and let him loose. He went directly to the mare and both animals pranced about, sniffing and nickering, side-stepping, and nudging and more. When the men saw the two knew what to do, they left the meadow, and went to the fire. Gabe poured the man a cup of coffee, and watched as he tried it, frowning. "What is this called?"

"Coffee, but you might like it better with some of this," suggested Gabe as he reached into the bag of sugar and put a bit in the man's cup.

Raven tasted it again, smiled, nodding, "It is good, this coffee."

"But you've never had it before?"

"One time, long ago, when a trader came from the south. He was not like you, darker, hair like mine, but not like his," nodding to Ezra.

"Probably Spanish. I saw the rifle you carried, it is Spanish, a musket. Did you get that from a trader?"

"No. I took it from a Comanche!" he spat. "But I have no power for it. I use it as a war club."

Gabe grinned, "I take it you don't have many traders come to trade with your people."

"No, they bring sickness and more. That is why my people were not trusting of you."

"I know what you mean. We just left a village of the Shoshone that had been made sick by the traders that came into their village. Three of their people crossed over before we were able to rid the village of the sickness."

White Raven frowned as he looked at Gabe, "Are you a medicine man?"

Gabe grinned, glanced at Ezra, "No, but my friend has done the work of a medicine man before, and more."

White Raven looked from Gabe to Ezra then back to Ezra, "Why is your skin so dark?"

Ezra chuckled, "That is the way of *my* people. We are all like this," he motioned to his skin and hair, "that is why they call me Black Buffalo."

"And you have the power of a medicine man?"

Ezra grinned, glanced to Gabe with a *Why'd you say that?* look, then answered, "Sometimes, yes. But I do not call myself a medicine man."

White Raven glanced from Gabe to Ezra and said, "It is good to learn these things. Do you trade with the people?"

"We have done some trading, but that is not why we are here. We just want to learn and know about the country and the people, like you," answered Gabe, then paused and thought, "Would you like to have what you need to use your rifle?"

"Do you have these things?"

"Of course, we need them for our rifles," answered Gabe as he rose to go to the packs. He fetched an extra horn of powder, a handful of patches and balls, and returned to the fire. He handed the gathered items to White Raven and asked, "Have you shot your rifle before?"

"Yes, until I had no more of these," he stated, lifting his hands up with the treasured items.

"Well, those balls are a little smaller than what you would use, but they'll do. You might have to use two," holding up two fingers, "patches to make it tight, but it'll shoot fine."

The men continued to visit, grinning as they heard a few squeals and snorts from the little meadow, and White Raven told them of the lay of the land in the direction they were traveling. "To the south, the people are the Mouache Ute and beyond them are the Kapota Ute." He paused as he looked at the men, stood and went to his horse to retrieve an item from his gear. When he returned he held out a wide beaded and decorated belt. He held it out to Gabe, "This is what some call a peace belt," he watched as Gabe gently fingered the decorations of beads, quills, and elk's teeth and more. "As you meet others of different bands, if you show this, they will know you are a friend."

Gabe looked up at White Raven, "This is beautiful!" he declared then with a thought, he went to his packs, returned and handed White Raven a necklace of grizzly bear claws and beads. The man's eyes flared, and he looked up at Gabe, frowned, and listened as Gabe said, "This is our gift to you. It doesn't say much like your gift does, but it is between friends."

White Raven knew it was a special gift for few are those who have killed a great bear and he held it with respectful hands, "Did you kill this bear?"

"Yeah, it was one of 'em. My woman made that necklace from its claws and," as he pointed to the necklace, "his teeth." Gabe glanced to Ezra and both men knew this was not the most treasured of Gabe's necklaces, but one made for a trade such as this.

"I will wear this with honor," declared White Raven.

As they rode from the camp, Gabe thought they were well prepared for the days ahead. They had added to their larder with two deer, stripped and smoked, and with a lot of information garnered from their visits with White Raven. He was a knowledgeable man and knew his country well. When Gabe explained their plan and purpose, he had given them as much detail about the country they would traverse as possible. "Three days south is a big river the Spanish call Colorado, that comes from the high mountains where the sun rises and goes through the mountains to the west. Cross the river and go south with these mountains," pointing to the beginning of the Sawatch mountains to the west, "always on this shoulder," tapping his right shoulder. "You will follow another small river until there is a valley where four rivers come together between the mountains. Follow the stream on this shoulder," again tapping his right shoulder, "that lies at the base of a narrow but very high mountain. You will go over a high trail and come to another long valley that follows a small river. Those are the Sawatch mountains."

"Sawatch in your tongue means 'blue earth spring', why are the mountains called that?"

White Raven grinned, stood, and pointed, "Are not the mountains, sky, and trees blue?"

Gabe chuckled, "Yup, guess they are at that. Just different shades of blue."

They had followed the words of White Raven and had a good three days of travel behind them when they stood at the banks of the Colorado River. The women declared they would stay by the river for a day of rest, to which Gabe replied, "Alright, but let's get to the other side before we make camp!" He led the way across the crooked stream they had followed from the north, went upstream on the Colorado about a half-mile before spotting a likely crossing, and nudged Ebony into the water and across. They rounded a bit of a knob at the end of a long finger ridge and dropped into the valley formed by the river they would soon follow further south. The smaller river bent back on itself forming a wide peninsula thick with grass and willows, but a clearing near the water sat in the shade of some inviting cottonwoods and the women stepped down and went to work to prepare their camp and give the children room to romp.

23 / GOLD

Capitan Francisco de Almeida was a proud man, believing that he was superior to the other men in the expedition by both position and birth, and now his group of prospectors had discovered a rich deposit of gold, proving his superiority. He stood before his men, gloating over his find of the day, "I have discovered the greatest deposit of all! We will start mining right away!" He looked at his lieutenant Diego Garcia, "You, Sergeant de Noli, and your men will start building rocker boxes and sluices! Sergeant Alvares, Sergeant Corte-Real, you and your men will start panning. Sergeant Fernandes, you and your men will move our camp nearer our gold mining. I will take my men and move upstream to find the source of the gold."

As they started to disperse, Diego spotted movement on the far side of the river and hissed at the others, motioning them to take cover. He looked at the Capitan, motioning to the river and both men, shielded by a tall ponderosa, watched a band of Indians, all mounted and numbering about twenty warriors, start through the brush at rivers edge, coming toward their camp.

The Capitan whispered, "Get the men stationed through the trees, along the edge and we will take them at my order!"

Diego frowned, "Do you not want to talk with them, Capitan?"

"I will talk, but we must show by force that we are to be obeyed!" he snarled as he watched the band come through the brush.

The Capitan had heard about some native people and how they painted themselves for battle, but not all did that, and these were not painted. They had mistakenly thought the Apache, far to the south would be painted, but they attacked and had the Spanish not been prepared, they would have lost the battle quickly. He would not make that mistake again, and this would be a good opportunity to capture some of the men and make slaves of them to work the streams and more for the gold they discovered.

Lieutenant Garcia quickly stationed the men along the tree line, cautioning them to stagger their firing. He came to the Capitan's side, whispered, "The men are ready, Capitan."

The Capitan grunted, slipping his matched pistols

from his bandolier, glanced at the beautiful weapons known as *Flintlocks a Las Tres Modas* and made by the noted Ybarzabel family. They had miquelet locks and were exquisitely inlaid with gold filagree. He shook his head that he had such weapons here in the wilderness among such common people and to fight against the barbarian natives.

When the natives came from the river, a simple hand motion from their leader prompted them to fan out to either side, forming a ragged skirmish line as they neared the tree line. When the line of mounted natives was within thirty yards, Capitan de Almeida stepped from behind the tree, his pistols held at his side, and stood before the leader, "Ho! I am Capitan Francisco de Almeida; I am in command of this exploration. Why do you approach our camp?" He spoke in Spanish, knowing no other language and in his arrogance believed that any leader should be conversant in the tongue of the superior people.

The leader nudged his mount forward a few steps, stopped, and glared at the man before him. He had seen the others in the trees, and his scouts had already told of their number and actions. He spoke in the language of his people, the Mouache Ute, and used sign, "I am Red Sleeves, in your tongue, Mangas Colorados. This is our land; you are not to be here!"

Francisco did not fully understand what the man said, but by the sign he used, he was certain the leader was saying they were not welcome. He was impressed by the man, tall, muscular, long black braids that fell over each shoulder, a bone hair-pipe breastplate with bright spots of beads or tufts of hair, a breechcloth with beaded designs and fringed buckskin breeches. The chief showed no fear, only anger as he glowered at the man.

Lieutenant Diego Garcia had come beside his Capitan and stood with his rifle held across his chest. He leaned closer to Francisco and said, "The men are ready, Capitan."

Francisco nodded, looked at the big Ute, slowly lifted his hand high as a signal to his men, then told the man, "You and your men are now my prisoners! You will do as I say, or you will be killed!" he spat the words, each one dripping with contempt.

Although the chief did not understand the words, he detected the meaning and turned to look at his men, but before he could speak, the Capitan dropped his arm and shouted, "Fire!" The woods erupted with thunder and smoke as a dozen rifles exploded. The barrage dropped three men from their horses, wounded two others that fell forward on the necks of their animals but grasped the manes to stay aboard. The chief was not hit and shouted to his men, "Now!" and they let loose a torrent of arrows, but their weapons were nothing in comparison with the rifles of the Spaniards.

The Capitan lifted his pistol, "Stop! You are my

prisoner," and walked toward the chief, his aim unwavering. The chief's eyes flared, and he lifted his lance as he dug heels to his mount and charged the Capitan. Francisco stood his ground and waited but an instant then dropped the hammer on his first pistol, the slug taking the chief at the base of his neck, splintering his bone hair-pipe necklace, and knocking the big man back, but he kept a tight hold on the rein and his lance, and with his last effort, fought to fling the lance toward the man before him. But his strength was gone, and the lance fluttered with the weak throw and fell to the ground but an instant before the chief landed on his face at the feet of his mount.

The others saw their chief fall and momentarily milled about, confused, until the Capitan shouted, "Do not move!" as he lifted his second pistol, holding it out before him, and shouted again, "NO!" The remaining Ute warriors, looked at the man, saw many others come from the trees, rifles held before them, and at the signal from the leader of the intruders, dropped their weapons and slipped from their horses. He nodded to Diego to subdue the captives. With barked commands, his men forced the Ute warriors to their knees and began binding them with braided rawhide tethers. Unseen by either the Capitan or Diego, amid the confusion one of the wounded warriors had run from the fight to return to his village and tell what had happened.

* * * * *

When the wounded warrior came into the village, his horse at a gallop, women and children scattered, some ran behind the warrior as he wound through the village, reining up his horse in the central compound before the lodge of the village chief. When the horse slid to a stop in a cloud of dust, many of the people gathered as the rider fell from his horse. A woman ran to his side, and lifted his head to her lap, speaking to him, but was stopped when the shadows of two of the village leaders came near. The leader, Stone Buffalo, stood beside the shaman, Black Calf, and looked at the man on the ground. "Why are you here?" asked the chief.

The wounded man groaned, his woman looked up at the chief, tears in her eyes, and the man struggled to speak, "Our warriors, many killed, others captured by the men who camp in the trees."

"You returned without your brothers, why?"

"To . . . warn," he coughed up blood, breathed deep and added, "you and the village. They fired without parley."

The chief glared at the man, motioned to the shaman to tend to him, then turned away, to summon the council.

"Most of our warriors were in that band!" declared one of the elders, "We have too few to send more, we must protect our village!"

"Yes! The buffalo come and we must have our hunt, or our people will die!" demanded another.

"We cannot sit here and do nothing," roared the chief, Stone Buffalo. "Are you women that you would let our men be made captives and killed and do nothing?"

"Perhaps when the other hunting parties return," began one of the more respected elders, a man with many years of leading the Ute warriors. Walks on Mountains paused, looking from one to the other of the council, so many were missing and were leading the hunting parties. The only leader who remained, Red Sleeves, had been sent to see about the intruders to the valley and now they were told he had been killed. "Those that remain, are old and not the warriors we once were. To go against these intruders only to be killed or captured as they were, would be foolish. We have two others who have been war leaders that now lead hunting parties. When they return, perhaps they will rescue the captives."

The others had fallen silent while the white-haired leader spoke, looking to one another when he paused, understanding the truth of his words. This village of thirty lodges had boasted of as many as fifty proven warriors, but in one day, that number had been halved and there would be weeping and wailing in several lodges this night. The old man looked around the circle of the council, saw none but old men, the youngest being the chief but even Stone Buffalo had white showing in his hair. Walks on Mountains continued, "I say, send one or two of our young men to watch these intruders, let them return and let us know who still lives and what is being done with the captives. And when our warriors return, then we can act and not leave the village in danger."

The council nodded, some beating the ground before them, others lifting hands high and shouting their war cries. But the chief stood, arms uplifted, "As always, the wise words of Walks on Mountains are good. Our blood runs hot with anger, sorrow, and a need for vengeance, but it would be best to wait for the others to return. It will be done!" At these words, the others nodded and rose to leave. The chief stepped outside and summoned several of the young men, all eager to prove themselves as warriors, and spoke to them. He admonished caution and the need to stay safe so they could report on what was happening to their warriors. When he finished, he sent one for his horse and sent him on his way.

24 / SAWATCH

"As you come to the confluence of many creeks, they are like your hand," White Raven held his hand before him, the back of his hand facing him. "There are many streams that come together, you are on this one," pointing to his wrist, "but when you leave this valley, you will take this one," pointing at the little finger on his right hand. "It will take you between the high mountains but stay on the main trail beside the creek. It will take you into the valley of the big mountains." Gabe was remembering what White Raven had told them about the trail they now followed.

They had traveled two days and were now mid-day of the third day. The valley before them was just as White Raven had described, many smaller valleys branched off, each with its own watershed and run-off creek, and the valley before them was like the palm of your hand. He nudged Ebony on the trail that rode the shoulder of a tall peak that stood high off their right shoulder. With the squared off top pushing above timber line and standing grey against the blue sky, he knew they were in the country of mighty mountains, more of them, and bigger ones than any they had seen before. He breathed deep of the crisp mountain air, tasting the sweetness of the pines and the bitter bite of the aspen, but filling his lungs with freedom. He smiled at the thought, prompting Cougar to ask, "What makes my husband smile?"

He chuckled deep in his chest, smiled at his woman, and answered, "Oh, just the beauty of the mountains, the fresh air, being here with the ones I love, just about everything!"

Cougar smiled and fidgeted in her seat, holding tight to Fox who was trying to snooze as he leaned against his mother, soaking up her warmth. She answered, "That is the way I feel also." As they rode she remembered the first time they rode together as man and wife and how strange she thought it was to be traveling with nowhere special to go nor purpose for going. But now, she reveled in the freedom they had to do as Gabe and Ezra had become accustomed to doing; exploring, and discovering new lands and new people. Before, as a war leader, whenever they left the village it was for a particular purpose, a raiding party, a rescue party, a hunt, or to move the village, or even to go the grand encampment, but never just to go with no purpose. But she had become as the others, happy to see new places and meet new people, each place, and each new people a great adventure.

The trail sided the creek as they pushed into the deep gorge between the towering mountains. Black timber climbed the steep sided slopes, most with as many rockslides as run-off gulches, but all standing tall and rugged with the grey granite peaks showing like the tips of lances trying to pierce the blue of heaven. The slopes on their right, or the north side of the trail, was painted in splotches of deep blue/green of the pines, spruces, and firs, intermittent with splashes of bright green foliage of the aspen. Time and again, ridges from the mountain tops appeared to push timber covered knobs into the valley, making the stream and trail veer around the rocky slopes. They passed a bit of a pond that nestled in a notch at the end of a long gulch, but it was too early to camp and they pushed on through the gorge. The trail made another swoop around a knob only to break into a wider valley, rich with beaver ponds and black timber fringed with aspen. When they came to a confluence of streams, one coming from a deep cut on the east edge, a grassy shoulder invited them to camp on the open slope overlooking the valley of beaver ponds.

The following day, with an early start, they pushed through the narrow canyon that opened up at the end of several finger ridges coming from the high mountains on the south side of the trail. The climb was steady, and the trail angled across the north face of a bald mountain to take them to the crest of the pass, only to drop them at an angle through the thick timber into the valley below that held the headwaters of another small river. Abundant with beaver ponds, the long valley led them south until it rounded the shoulder of the long line of mountains riding the high side on the west. They could see the mouth of the valley about three miles before them, but Gabe looked at Ezra, frowning, and Ezra nodded. The trail widened and Gabe motioned Cougar alongside, and Ezra and Dove came up behind them. Gabe twisted in his seat to look at Ezra, and his friend responded, "Yup," took a deep breath that lifted his shoulders, then added, "Tain't right." It was not uncommon for Ezra to get a premonition of danger, and often Gabe had a similar sense. It did not need commenting as each man understood the other and the gift of Ezra, gained from his Black Irish mother with her Celtic and Druid family ties, was the greater.

"Let's go closer to the mouth, and I'll climb high and have a better look-see."

"Sounds 'bout right. In the meantime, loosen your rifle an' such."

Gabe understood his friend to say, "Make ready, trouble's coming," and reached for his rifle to limber it in the scabbard, making certain it would slip freely out if needed. He reached forward and lifted the saddle pistols, freeing them as well. It was common, especially for the saddle pistols, with the rocking gait of the horses, for the weapons to slip tightly into the leather scabbard or holsters, and become bound up, making added effort necessary to free them. But once slipped free, it would take some time for the weapons to repeatedly bounce and slide deeper in the flexible leather.

The trail had stayed off the north bank of the little river, keeping close to the timberline and away from any bogs or beaver ponds, and as they neared the wide mouth of the canyon, Gabe motioned the group into the trees at the skirt of the mountain. He stepped down, helped Bobcat down, then took Fox from Cougar, and slipped his rifle from the scabbard. He looked at Ezra, "You comin'?"

"You need to ask?" responded Ezra, slipping his Lancaster rifle from the scabbard. Both men regularly carried a Bailes over/under double barreled pistol in their belt, a tomahawk, knives, and their necessary accoutrements for their weapons. Both men looked at the women, "We'll be back soon," stated Gabe and with a motion to Wolf to stay with the women and children, they started across the narrow valley, picking their way between the beaver ponds, willows, and alders. Once across they started up the steep slope of the tall mountain at the end of the valley, having chosen it with its bald south facing slope that faced the broad valley of the Arkansa.

They had to zig-zag up the steep mountainside, moving from thick oak brush to random juniper or stunted piñon, trying not to expose themselves to any unwanted company. With continual looks over their shoulders, Gabe finally came to a halt in the shadow of a lone fir tree and sat down to have his look-see. He slipped the scope from the case and stretched it out as Ezra said, "Is that smoke yonder? There at the end of those trees on the other side of the valley."

Gabe lifted the scope to scan the area where Ezra pointed, paused, moved it slowly back and forth, "Yeah, looks like it, but whatever its coming from is on the other side of that low ridge. All I can see is smoke, but I'd guess that's an Indian village."

Gabe sat with knees up, elbows on his knees to stabilize the scope, and continued his search of the valley. Maybe it was the village that had give them both that tingling feeling that rode their spine and was usually a precursor of some kind of danger, but Gabe wasn't ready to settle for that explanation. He kept looking. He searched the far timber near the smoke, saw a long narrow lake that lay in the trees, but nothing else. He brought the scope closer and followed the meandering course of the river and it disappeared in the far reaches of the broad valley, then brought the scope closer. He looked to his right, upstream on the river, over the slight hump at the end of the long ridge and saw an expansive green valley and what he thought was a herd of elk grazing in the tall grass. With a cursory look at the valley, he brought the scope back to the south and looked at the broad flat alluvial plain that lay before the mountain where they sat. He could make out the course of a small stream, several small clearings among the smattering of timber and there, in a bit of a clearing along the creek, several horses and what appeared to be several men, working along the creek.

He took a deep breath, making Ezra look toward him, then focused the scope again, and leaned into his knees, unconsciously wanting to get closer, and slowly moved the scope, scanning the exposed flat and creek to see everything possible. "If that's what I think it is, it ain't good!" he declared, lowering the scope to hand it to Ezra. He pointed and described, "There on that flat, where it opens up a little and the creek flows through it. Several horses and men."

Ezra focused the scope, slowly moving it to see what had alarmed Gabe, then stopped, stared, and dropped the scope. "Looks to me like their workin' the stream, prob'ly lookin' for gold. I'm guessin' Spanish, but they're usin' Indians to work, an' I just saw one of 'em take a whippin'!"

25 / ALLIES

They made their way off the bald face of the mountain, careful to move from brush to trees, always conscious of their visibility, fleeting though it was, but as they neared the thicker trees at the flank of the mountain, Ezra put out a hand to stop their movement. He nodded to the trees, bent to the side to see better, and whispered, "Horses, two of 'em. Tethered in the trees. Somebody's up to somethin'."

Gabe looked around, "Let's wait 'em out," he whispered, nodding to a thick cluster of fir near some tall spruce. They carefully worked toward the dark timber, watching for the return of the riders. When they settled down to wait, Gabe said, "Those are Indian mounts, and I'm guessing their checking on their friends with the prospectors."

"That would mean they're prob'ly from the village across the valley. But if that village is very large, why haven't they recovered their people?" asked Ezra.

"Guess we'll just have to wait and see."

A short while later, the watchful eye of Ezra caught movement in the trees and hissed at Gabe, nodding toward the horses. "I think somebody's comin'."

Two young warriors stealthily came through the thickest of the timber, wending their way between the close-growing trees, and reached for the tethers on their horses. As they freed the animals and started to swing aboard, they were stopped by the softly spoken words of Gabe, as he spoke in Shoshone, believing they would probably understand at least the gist of what he was saying, "Do not move." The two men froze, hands at the withers of their horses, bows in their quivers at their backs.

"Turn around and face us."

The two warriors slowly turned to face the men behind them. They frowned at the sight of Ezra, probably having never seen a man of his color before, and both looked at Gabe, eyes wide, a mixture of anger and fear showing in their expressions.

Gabe lowered his rifle, stood it butt down on his foot, and spoke, "We are not like those," nodding to the trees where the young warriors had come from, "we are friends of the Ute people. Why are you here?"

The two looked to one another and the taller of the two answered, "We were told to scout the men that held our warriors and report back to our village."

"And what did you find?"

"The men that have our warriors are not like you, they are dark, but not like him," pointing at Ezra with his chin, "but our men are tied together, and beaten and made to do the work of their captors."

"How long have they been held?"

"Three days."

"Why does your village do nothing to free the warriors?"

"Most of the warriors are gone on the hunt to the south, looking for buffalo."

Gabe glanced at Ezra, then asked, "How many men hold your warriors?"

The young man flashed both hands, all fingers extended, twice, to indicate twenty.

"Those men, do they have many of these?" asked Gabe, lifting his rifle before them.

"Yes, they have many. And they have those," pointing at the pistol at Gabe's belt, "also."

Gabe stepped back, "Go, tell your leaders what you have found. Tell them we," motioning to Ezra with a nod, "and our families will come to your village and will help your people free your warriors."

The two young men looked at one another, slowly turned to mount and once aboard, they looked at the two men before them, frowned and slowly rode away and through the trees at the edge of the river.

"I knew it, I knew it!" declared Ezra, "You always

do it!"

Gabe frowned at his friend, "What are you talkin' about?"

"It don't matter where we go, when it is, or how remote it may be, you always find somebody needin' help or somethin' that gets us into another fight!" He started in the direction of the river, "And I don't know why I keep hangin' around! I swear, you're gonna be the death of me!" he mumbled as he walked ahead, shaking his head as he pushed through the brush. Gabe chuckled at the usual antics of his friend, but also knew Ezra would never leave his side.

"So, what if those prospectors catch sight of us? Ya think maybe we should wait till after dark?" asked Ezra as they started to mount up.

"I think they're too busy digging for gold to pay much attention to anything else. Besides, we wouldn't be a threat to them, travelin' with our families and such. We'll just follow the river, move across the valley and into the trees below that little lake yonder. I'm thinkin' the Ute are camped below the lake, at least that's where we saw the smoke."

"We'll I'm ridin' with my rifle right'chere!" he declared, nodding to his rifle that lay across his pommel. His son, Chipmunk, sat behind him and he didn't want anything to hinder his access to his weapon.

"Likewise," answered Gabe, nodding to his own

rifle that lay exposed as it rested on the pommel of his saddle.

With Gabe in the lead, the entourage of families stayed with the trail that shouldered the river, but well above the marshy lands with the willows, bogs and more. As the valley opened to longer valley running north and south, lying in the lap of the tallest mountains of the Sawatch range, they pushed across the grassy flat and followed a slight game trail through the thickets of brush siding the feeder creek that met the river. Once through the brush, Gabe kept to the game trail siding the long timbered ridge below the lake. When they crested the ridge, Gabe was surprised to see the crescent shaped lake was smaller than he first imagined. The upper end lay in the narrow valley with the run-off creek feeding it, and bent around the point, with the same creek as the outlet. The timbered hills dropped to water's edge of the lake Gabe guessed to be less than a mile at its longest point. Its cerulean waters were inviting, and Ezra said, "I'll betcha there's some mighty fine fish in there!"

Gabe spotted a clearing on the lower end of the lake, nodded in that direction, "Let's make camp there."

"I thought we were goin' to the village?" asked Ezra.

"Yeah, but, it might be better if you and I go alone. Don't wanna get us in a fix we can't get out of, ya reckon?"

"Yeah, I s'pose they might be kinda testy what with

their men taken captive and such."

It was late afternoon, and the sun was dropping toward the high mountain tops when Gabe readied his gear to go to the village. Cougar came to his side, "I believe I should go with you. I understand their tongue better and can speak for you."

Gabe paused, frowning, looking at his woman. "Yeah, you're prob'ly right about that, but what about the young'uns?" he asked, already knowing she would have spoken to Dove about the little ones, but he was searching for a reason to leave her behind. He had the tendency to always want to protect her, as he should, but her nature and experience as a war leader was to confront danger straight on and not allow others to stand before her.

She smiled at him, slightly shaking her head, "They will be fine with Dove and Ezra."

"So, we're leaving him behind also?"

She pursed her lips and shrugged as she stepped near her appaloosa, tightening the girth before stepping into the stirrup. Gabe shook his head, grinning, knowing he had already lost the argument. He swung aboard Ebony, motioned for Wolf to come with them, and they started down the narrow game trail toward the village.

It was only about two miles to the village, and they had no sooner broken from the trees than the alarm was sounded, and people scattered to their lodges.

The two young warriors they met in the trees stood before them, arrows nocked, blocking their way into the camp. Cougar stood in her stirrups, "We come in peace. We would speak to your leaders about the men in the valley who have your warriors!" Although the words were in the tongue of the Ute, which was very similar to that of the Shoshone, Gabe understood most of what she said.

The same warrior that spoke in the trees answered, "Step down, we will take you to our chief." With their attention on the two mounted visitors, the young warriors had not seen Wolf until Gabe stepped down and Wolf came from behind Ebony to stand beside him. The young men stepped back, eyes wide and frowning as they looked from Gabe to the wolf beside him, but when Gabe put his hand on the scruff of Wolf's neck and spoke to him, they looked at the white man and motioned for them to follow.

They followed the two young men, leading their horses and with Wolf between them, into the central compound of the village. Two men, standing with stoic expressions showing above their folded arms, watched as they neared. Gabe guessed them to be the chief and shaman, but listened as the young man spoke, motioning toward Gabe and Cougar, "This is one of the men we saw, the dark one is not here."

The older of the two men motioned the warriors aside, and glared at Gabe and Cougar, with but a glance at Wolf. "I am Stone Buffalo, the leader of this village, this," without a glance nor motion toward the man who sided him, "is Black Calf, our shaman. Why are you here?"

Gabe answered in English, letting Cougar interpret, "I am Spirit Bear, and my wife is Cougar Woman of the Tukkutikka Shoshone. We came from the village of White Raven of the Yapudttka Ute," he paused and handed the beaded belt given him by White Raven, "we are friends of the Ute people, and have come to see this great land and to meet the people."

Stone Buffalo examined the belt, handed it to the shaman, and asked, "What have you to do with the men that have taken my warriors?"

"Nothing. We do not know these men, but we saw them beating one of your warriors as the others were bound and made to work. We saw this before meeting your warriors in the trees."

"Hawk that Screams," started the chief, nodding to the young man beside him, "told us that you wanted to help us against these men."

"That is true. But only if you want us to do this."

Stone Buffalo looked from Gabe to Cougar Woman, frowned at her and spoke to her, "Our people have not been friends. There have been times when our people have fought one another, and you are with this man who says he will help us."

Gabe spoke up, "We do not care about what has

happened in the past. We are here as friends and it is what we," motioning to himself and the chief, "do now that matters." He paused, glanced at Cougar Woman, and nodded.

She spoke for herself, "I am Cougar Woman, a war leader of the Tukkutikka Shoshone. Our people live far to the north of your people, and our people have not been friends. But now, others have taken warriors of the people and beat them and kill them. This we cannot allow."

The chief cocked one eyebrow up as he looked at the woman before him, "Your words are true." He looked at Gabe, "I will speak to our council, and we will decide." He turned to a woman that stood nearby, motioned to her to come near, "This is my woman, Red Beaver, she will feed you while you wait, and we will talk again."

Cougar spoke up, "I must see to my family. We are camped near the lake," motioning behind them, "if you would speak with us, we will be there." The chief frowned, unaccustomed to being refused, but with a glance to Gabe, he nodded and turned away to enter his lodge. Gabe frowned at Cougar, who showed a slight smile as she mounted the appaloosa, "I will explain."

As they left the village, Gabe led the way and at the first wide spot in the trail he stopped, waited for her to come alongside, and said, "Alright, explain. I didn't think it customary to refuse the request of the chief."

"It is not. But he must understand we are not his warriors nor his people and are worthy of the respect of an equal. Now to speak to us, he must come to our camp as we came to his."

Gabe slowly nodded, then shook his head as they started up the trail to return to their camp.

As expected, it was the next morning before Stone Buffalo rode into their camp, and surprising to Gabe and company, he was accompanied by his wife, Red Beaver, and the young warrior, Hawk that Screams. Gabe welcomed them into the camp, asked them to step down and motioned them to the log by the fire. Ezra stepped forward as Gabe introduced him, speaking in Shoshone, knowing Cougar would translate, "This is my brother, Black Buffalo, and his wife, Grey Dove of the Kuccuntikka Shoshone." He motioned to Cougar to come near with their youngest, "And this is our youngest son, Fox, and our other son is there on the robe, Bobcat. He is with Black Buffalo's son, Chipmunk and daughter, Squirrel."

The chief stepped forward, looked at Ezra and Dove, "I am Stone Buffalo, the leader of our village of the Mouache Ute people." He spoke the dialect of the Ute, but his was so much like the Shoshone, he was easily understood. "This is my wife, Red Beaver, and our son," nodding to the young warrior, "Hawk that Screams."

Cougar nodded toward Red Beaver, then looked at Stone Buffalo, "Will you honor us by joining us for a meal?"

Stone Buffalo grinned, "We would like that." He nodded to his wife, and she smiled and went to help the women.

The men sat down, Gabe and Ezra picking up their cups of steaming coffee and Gabe offered one to Stone Buffalo. When he accepted the cup from Gabe, he sipped at it and grinned, nodded, then began, "I spoke with our council. We believe it would be best to wait for the return of our hunting parties before we go against those who have taken our warriors. You have three warriors, and we have but young men who have yet to be proven in battle. Those who have taken our men have many weapons of thunder and are without honor."

"When do you expect your hunters to return?" asked Ezra.

"Any day. We sent men to bring them home soon, but we are not certain where they hunt. If it is a good hunt, it would take longer, but if our young men find them, then perhaps they will return soon."

"Will you have scouts to watch the camp of the

prospectors?" asked Gabe.

"Prospec . . . what is this word?"

"Prospectors, uh, in your language it would mean those who dig in the ground."

The chief slowly nodded, then answered, "They will always be watched. Our young men watch from different places, but they are always watched."

Gabe glanced to Ezra, nodding slowly, "Perhaps we will also scout their diggings. The more we know, the better we can fight them."

"Yes, that is good."

"If something were to happen that we could not wait for the hunters to return, would there be many of your people that could join in the fight?"

"We have many old men, and young men. The old could fight, but . . ." he shrugged. "And the young are unproven. Our council has spoken to the people and they are ready to defend our village, but to go to fight would not be good. It would leave our village without protection."

"I understand," answered Gabe, then looked at Hawk that Screams, "If you had to fight, how many of your friends would you trust to fight with you?"

The young man glanced at his father, then looked at Gabe as he sat up straight, "There are three, maybe four, that I would be proud to fight with."

Cougar, Dove and Red Beaver came close with platters and more of food. They served the men and

Cougar stepped behind her man, looked at Stone Buffalo, "I have known of my man, and Black Buffalo," nodding toward Ezra, "to take on as many as there are there," pointing with her chin toward the valley, "and destroy them all!" She paused, "They are great warriors and have fought the Hidatsa, the Piikani Blackfoot, the Liksiyu, and the Absáalooke, and many bad men that say they are traders! I have seen my man stand before the great grizzly, the cougar of the mountains, and more!"

Grey Dove would not be outdone, stood behind Ezra and added, "These men, Spirit Bear and Black Buffalo, have fought with many native peoples, the Osage, the Otoe and Omaha, the Arapaho, the Kutenai, the Nez Percé, and the Shoshone. They are friends with many and brothers with most!"

Everyone stood silent for just a moment, until Gabe spoke softly, "And we would be friends with the Mouache Ute also."

"So be it!" declared Stone Buffalo, then lifted his trencher plate and began eating. The others grinned and joined in to quickly finish off the prepared meal and sat back to learn about one another. Stone Buffalo began with, "I have heard of many of the people your woman," nodding to Ezra, "spoke of, but some I do not know. Who are those she said were," he paused as he thought of her words, "Osage?"

Gabe grinned, "Do you know of the great river

that runs from the north to the south and is called by some, the Mississippi?"

Stone Buffalo frowned, shook his head. "I know of no such river. Where is it found?"

"Many moons to the rising of the sun, there is a great river. Beyond that river is the land of other peoples like you, the Shawnee, Cherokee, Chickasaw, and more. But many white men, like me, have come from across the great waters and now live in the land where the Shawnee and others once lived." He continued his story of the history of the white man's incursion on the land of the natives and told of their coming beyond the great river. He spoke well into the late morning, until one of the scouts came to their camp, seeking the chief.

Stone Buffalo stood when the young warrior called Spotted Deer stepped down from his mount and came near. "Our hunters will return soon. They will be here yet this day, perhaps after the sun leaves the sky."

"Who is the leader?" asked Stone Buffalo.

"Little Bull," answered Spotted Deer. "They have taken much game also."

"Good, good." He turned to look at Gabe, "Little Bull is the war leader of our people. He is a great warrior and those with him are proven warriors."

"How many does he bring?" asked Gabe.

"Three hands, maybe a few more."

Gabe grinned, "Good, good," he paused, looked

from the chief to Ezra, "That will give us time to scout out the prospectors." Ezra nodded, turned away to go to the horses and make ready.

"When your men return, send someone to tell us and we will join you for a war council," suggested Gabe.

The chief nodded, looked up to see his son had already retrieved their horses, and accepted the rein of his mount. He glanced to see Red Beaver saying her goodbyes to her new friends, then swung aboard his tall paint gelding. "We will talk soon."

Gabe looked at Ezra, then spoke to both Ezra and the women, "We will go to the crest, there," nodding to the long ridge that stood between them and the long valley below. "Depending on what we see, we might have to ride across the valley for a closer look. But it shouldn't take too long."

Cougar and Dove nodded, trusting their men to soon return, but knowing that anytime they left, they might not ever be seen again. The couples embraced, and with rifles and the telescope in hand, the men started through the trees to mount the ridge beyond the camp. They took to the highest point of the ridge, but soon realized they were too far away to get the view they needed. If there was going to be a battle, they had to know more. With a nod to one another, they returned to the camp to saddle up and make their scout.

When Cougar came near, Gabe explained, "Where the prospectors are working, and the Ute are being used, is too far for us to see well from here." He bent down and drew in the dirt, "This is the ridge there," nodding above their camp, "the wide flat that comes from the mountain is here and spread out across the edge of the valley where the river cuts through. The men are working in a wide gulch that runs this away," drawing a long line from the mountains to the river and coursing through the alluvial plain on the south edge. "We'll take cover in the trees here," jabbing his stick to the north of the gulch, "and watch until we have a good idea what's going on." He stood, shrugged, and turned to mount Ebony, but before he could, Cougar turned him back and embraced him. She stepped back, smiling, and said, "Return to me."

"Oh, I will, I will," laughed Gabe, pulling her close for another hug before he mounted Ebony to follow Ezra from the camp.

They retraced their route that brought them from the river below, crossed the shallow stream and went into the trees. With the thick growing fir trees, they had to pick their way carefully, but worked their way nearer the camp of the prospectors. When they were near enough to hear the noises of the workers, but still within the black timber, they stepped down, tethered the horses, and started their stalk of the gulch where they worked.

27 / PROSPECTORS

Diego struggled with his part in the captivity and enslavement of the natives. His own family had been in bondage before Diego became a man and the scars still reminded him of what slavery did to families. He knew that the trade of Native slaves had been outlawed by Governor Esteban Rodriguez Miró, but before they shipped out from Spain, word had spread about New Spain being traded back to the French. With the recent Revolutionary war in America, the changing of rule in what they had known as New Spain or Spanish Louisiana, the recent rebellion among the Louisiana planters that had become known as the Pointe Coupée conspiracy where twenty-three had been hanged, Diego had become incensed with any idea of slavery. But now, he had been made a part of the very thing he hated.

When he saw Capitan de Almeida returning from

his upstream search, he confronted him, "Capitan, I think what we are doing is wrong!"

The Capitan frowned as his Lieutenant, "What? What is wrong? We are getting gold and we will get much more! The men are working hard and with the slaves doing so much, what can be wrong?"

"The Indians, mi Capitan. What we do is not allowed by the decree of the governor!"

The Capitan scowled at Diego, looked at the workers laboring at the sluices and rockers, then back at Diego. "Do you not want a share of the gold, Diego?"

"Of course, mi Capitan, but . . ."

"Do you see any soldados, or the governor?" he said as he waved his arms around to indicate the land before them. "Who is to tell us what we must do?"

"What if the people of the village come for their men, do we kill them all?"

"If we have to, *si.* These people are nothing! Barbarians! Do you want to work the shovels and do all the digging, move all the dirt, and more, just to let these, these," he stuttered as he searched for the words, "these animals do nothing? They are no different than the mules that carry our goods! They are here to serve us!" He shook his head, started off, then turned back, "Unless you want to give your rank to one of the sergeants, or you want to work the rockers yourself, then get these foolish thoughts out of your *cabeza*!" He shook his head as he stomped off, grumbling.

As the Capitan passed Sergeant Alvares, he saw one of the Indians sit down, while the others worked. The Capitan hollered, "Sergeant! Give that man ten lashes!" The sergeant jumped, ran to the stack of gear, and snatched up the black snake bullwhip and laid the lash across the man's back. The Indian jumped to his feet facing the sergeant, saw the lash coming at him again and ducked to the side, grabbing the lash, and jerking it from the sergeant's hand. He reached for the hand grip, started toward Alvares, but within the first two steps, the blast from the pistol in the hand of the Capitan staggered him as he grabbed at his side. He brought up his hand, saw the blood and lay the whip out, bringing his arm back, the lash whispering through the air overhead as he glared at the Capitan, but the second pistol appeared in de Almeida's hand and bucked as it roared. The ball took the Indian in the middle of his solar plexus, driving him back and dropping him to the ground. He landed in a seated position, his chin dropping to his chest.

The Capitan immediately started reloading his pistols, looking around wide-eyed at the other Indians, some of whom strained at their bonds, and he barked to the sergeant, "Alvares, get your whip and lay it across the back of any Indian that moves!"

Alvares grabbed the bullwhip from the ground beside the dead Indian, coiled it and looked at each of the workers, then with a practiced hand, brought the whip through the air over his head and lay it out behind him, letting it trail after him as he snarled and stalked among the captives. He pointed and barked orders, driving the men back to their tasks.

His pistols reloaded, the Capitan replaced them in his bandolier, hollered for Diego, "Lieutenant!" and waited for the man to come before him. "I will take a crew and start excavation of the upper end of the gulch there," pointing to the branch gulch about a mile above the current diggings. "You keep these men working! With three sluices and four rockers, we should bring in a lot more gold if you keep them busy!"

"If we work them any harder, mi Capitan, we will kill them!"

"It does not matter! We will get more from the village!" he hollered over his shoulder as he strode away.

Diego went to the side of Sergeant Alvares, "One day . . ." he grumbled as he stared at the back of the Capitan.

"When?" asked the Sergeant, for they had talked about this before.

Diego looked at Alvares, "Soon, soon!" he reached down at the edge of the stack of gear, picked up one of the leather pouches with gold, and hefted it to judge the weight. The pouch was about the size of a man's forearm, and the one he held was half full of gold dust and nuggets. "When we have one of these, just like this which is about 12 to 15 Libra," he spoke as he lifted the pouch, knowing a Libra was about the same as an American pound, "for every man that is with us, then we will be ready!" Alvares let a smile split his face, as he nodded agreement, lust and greed showing in his eyes.

Diego started up the gulch to check on all the workers and equipment. The sluices were spaced out at each bend of the creek, making it easier to divert the water into the long boxes with the ripples in the bottom. Each sluice had a crew of both Spaniards and natives. The natives were shoveling the soil into the sluice, the Spaniards picking out the nuggets and moving and pushing the soil along with the current of the water. Where a sluice was not suitable, a crew was busy using a rocker box, one native shoveling the soil, two Spanish working the rocker box and water to wash the gravel, pick the nuggets, and periodically emptying the finer dust.

The crews were working well, although grumbling could be heard among both the natives and the Spaniards. Diego watched the Capitan leave with his crew of Sergeant Fernandes and three natives and four men of the expedition. They trailed two pack mules loaded with gear and soon disappeared up the gulch toward their excavation at the upper end of the smaller gulch and just past the fork. Diego breathed a sigh of relief, knowing they would be free of the taskmaster for the rest of the day, and he took advantage of the moment to find himself a seat in the shade where he could watch over the workers at his leisure.

Gabe and Ezra had watched the exchange between the Capitan and his men, and the subsequent shooting of the Ute warrior. When they saw the man fall, Gabe had to put his hand on Ezra's shoulder to restrain him, for they both knew that any intervention on their part now would be deadly for them. Ezra breathed deep, shaking his head and mumbling, but remained on his knee, watching the workers by the boxes and sluices. Gabe said, "I think we've seen enough here, but I don't know if we can get a look at the site that other bunch went to on up the gulch. There's not much cover on that side."

Ezra stood behind the big ponderosa, looked at Gabe, "Well, we could either go around up high, or down the valley and back through the timber. Either way would take a spell."

"Yeah, and I think we need to get back to camp. The huntin' party might be back and Stone Buffalo might be wantin' to meet up."

They moved back away from the diggings, working their way to the horses. When further from the site, Gabe said, "I think there's a big moon tonight, so if we have to, we can take a look at the other location by moonlight."

"Won't be the same without seein' how many workers and where they are," replied Ezra.

"Well, you always like surprises, so maybe you

can take that bunch," challenged Gabe, glancing at his friend.

As they stepped aboard their horses, Ezra answered, "You know, that might not be a bad idea, especially if that popinjay in charge is with that bunch. I'd like to put the measure to him with my war club."

Gabe shook his head chuckling as they rode from the trees to take the trail across the river and back to camp. It was late afternoon when they rode back into their camp to be greeted by the older boys who were playing at standing guard over their village. Chipmunk stepped before them, held up his lance and said, "Why are you here?"

"Ho! Don't shoot! We're friendly! Honest!" declared Ezra, holding his hands high and doing his best to keep from laughing.

Chipmunk looked from the men to Bobcat, then asked again, "Why are you here," trying to lower his voice and sound gruff.

Gabe, hands high, said, "We have come to eat! Are your women good cooks?"

Bobcat laughed, "No. They cannot cook anything! You have to cook your own food!"

The men stepped down and Gabe said to the women, "Did you hear what he said?"

Cougar Woman answered, as she stood hands on hips and scowling, "If you don't like my cooking, then cook it yourself!"

"So that's where he gets it!" answered Gabe, turning away to lead Ebony to the edge of the trees and picket him with the others. Ezra came beside him, chuckling, "I'm thinkin' the women have been teaching the young'uns a little rebellion, ya reckon?"

"Ummhmm, but what're we gonna do? Can't whip 'em, cuz they'd fight back! Can't get rid of 'em, cuz then we'd really have to eat our own cookin' and I remember havin' to do that."

Ezra laughed, "It's like I heard my pa say, 'Can't live with 'em, can't live without 'em."

28 / GROUNDWORKS

"My father asks that you come to our camp. Our war leader, Little Bull, and his men have returned, and my father asks for you and the council to meet," stated Hawk that Screams as he sat astride his horse at the edge of their camp.

Gabe and Ezra stood side by side before the young warrior, looked at one another, then back to Hawk. "Tell your father we will come right away," declared Gabe.

"It is good," declared Hawk as he jerked the head of his horse around and dug heels to the animal's ribs to return to the village.

The men quickly saddled the horses, made the usual check of their weapons, embraced the women, and swung aboard. The short distance took but a few minutes and they were greeted by both Hawk that Screams and his friend, Spotted Deer. They took the men's horses and pointed them to the lodge of Stone Buffalo, where other men were gathering. As they neared, the chief stepped forward to greet them and usher them into his lodge where the council would meet. One warrior stood as they entered, glaring at the intruders, until Stone Buffalo spoke, "This is Spirit Bear and Black Buffalo. They are friends and said they will fight with us against those who have taken our men as captives." He paused, looked from Gabe and Ezra to the intimidating man that stood before them. He was the same height as Gabe, muscled like Ezra, and the scars told of the man's experience in battle. With long braids that hung over his shoulders, three notched feathers in a top knot at the back of his head, a hair pipe bone breastplate that did nothing to mask his muscular chest, and a beaded breech cloth with fringed buckskins, he stood before them with a skeptical scowl. He glanced at Stone Buffalo as the chief said, "This is Little Bull, war leader of our people." Gabe and Ezra nodded as they stood with stoic expressions, with neither man nor Little Bull wavering in their stare at one another. Stone Buffalo added, "Be seated, we will talk," and motioned Gabe and Ezra to be seated opposite Stone Buffalo and Black Calf, with Little Bull taking his place on the other side of the chief.

Stone Buffalo began by explaining what the young scouts had reported as they watched the men in the valley after the warriors had become captives. He told of the numbers of the Spaniards, the remaining warriors, and the work that was done. As he finished, he looked to Gabe, "Is there anything else that must be said?"

"Yes," began Gabe, "we scouted the camp today. Another of your warriors was killed by the man that leads those below. They have divided their number, with this many," holding up nine fingers, "three of those were warriors, going into another gulch further up from the first."

At the report of another of their warriors being killed, much grumbling filled the lodge, but quickly quieted as Gabe continued. "The leader of that group is the chief of the Spaniards, the men that have taken your warriors."

Little Bull snarled and came to his feet, "Who are these that come to our council and dare to speak to our leaders? These could be against us and telling those that have taken our warriors what we plan! They cannot be trusted!" He sought to intimidate the visitors with his bluster and his stance, his feet wide and hands at his sides, fingers flexing and the muscles in his jaw rippling as he clenched his teeth. He stared at Gabe with a challenge in his eyes, his nostrils flaring as he breathed deep, flexing the muscles in his chest and shoulders.

Gabe grinned, one eyebrow raised, and looked

away from the man to the others about the circle. Stone Buffalo spoke with the authority of the chief of the village, "You will not insult the guests of my lodge! These men are here at my request! I am convinced they are friends of the *Mouache* as they were friends of the *Yapudttka.* Spirit Bear has said our friend are his friends, and our enemies are his enemies!" The admonishment from his chief cowered the war leader, who glared around the circle, then took his seat beside the chief.

Stone Buffalo also looked around the circle, then looked at Gabe, "Do you know these men that dig in the ground?"

"I do not know *these* men, but I know of others like them. They seek gold, the yellow stone that is found in the rivers and the mountains, like the yellow metal you have hanging on your breast plate," nodding to the chief. Gabe had noticed the gold nugget that decorated the center of the breast plate of the chief and knew the Ute knew something of the metal. "Among these people, the yellow stone is greatly desired and makes a man very wealthy, much like a warrior with many horses and wives. But these men also fight among themselves as they fight over this metal and against one another because they have taken the Ute warriors captive."

The chief frowned, his expression asking for a greater explanation, and Gabe continued. "When we scouted their camp today, and the chief of the men killed your warrior, it caused the others to talk with one another, and we could tell there were some that did not like what their chief did when he killed your warrior."

"Did they do anything to the chief because he killed the warrior?" asked the grey-haired man that sat beside the shaman.

Gabe glanced at the older man and answered, "They did not. I think they were as fearful of their leader as were the captives. The chief had ordered the warrior to be whipped but your warrior would not take that, tried to attack the man with the whip, but was killed by the chief."

The grey haired elder spoke again, "I am Walks on Mountains." He paused, then continued, "Do you believe the captives could be taken?"

Gabe looked at Little Bull, "How many proven warriors do *you* have?"

Little Bull flashed both hands, all fingers extended, twice, without speaking, but with a grunt.

"Would your young warriors join us?" Gabe asked of Stone Buffalo.

"Yes, that would give about one hand, or more, to help in the battle," answered the chief.

"Then yes, I believe we could take back your warriors, if Little Bull leads your men in this battle." Little Bull sat erect, one eyebrow lifted as he glared at this white man, yet proud that he had been recognized as the leader of the coming battle.

Walks on Mountains spoke again, "I say our warriors should move at first light to bring our men back, and that Little Bull and Spirit Bear lead in this vengeance quest!"

The other members beat the ground before them with the flat side of their war hawks or knives, some with fists balled up, but all shouted as they showed their agreement. Gabe glanced at those around the circle, letting his eyes fall on Little Bull then Stone Buffalo. The chief stood, "Then Little Bull and Spirit Bear and Black Buffalo will stay with Walks on Mountains and this chief to plan for the battle!"

Again the council voiced their agreement as they pounded the ground and spoke their support. When the noise subsided, the others rose to leave the lodge and let the warriors make their plans. One other warrior, who had sat silent through the talk, stayed behind, taking a seat beside Little Bull, and waited for the others to begin.

Walks on Mountains asked Gabe to tell of his scout, giving the details of the camp, the workers, the location, and number of workers and more. Gabe used a stick to draw a crude map in the dirt floor, pointing out the camp at the edge of the trees, where their horses were kept, how many workers, both Spaniard and native, labored in the stream and more. When he finished, the older man stared at the map, thought long about the numbers and looked at Little Bull, "Do you want to take this group with more numbers, or this group," pointing to the upper gulch, "where the chief of the diggers works?"

With no hesitation, Little Bull jabbed his finger in the dirt, "Here! Where their chief can be found!"

Walks on Mountains looked from Gabe to Ezra, asked, "Will you be with Spirit Bear or will you go with Little Bull?" Ezra glanced at Gabe, showing a slight nod then looked back at Walks, "I will go with Little Bull." The older warrior nodded, having detected the slight nod between the men and suspecting that Black Buffalo wanted a chance at the chief of the diggers. He glanced at Gabe, "This man," nodding to the warrior beside Little Bull, "is Rock that Roars. He has been a war leader, is a great warrior. He will be with you as you take these," pointing to the larger group that labored in the lower gulch.

The men continued talking of the coming fight, working out as many details and possibilities as could be considered. As the conversation continued, the animosity between the men seemed to wane and their respect for one another grew. As they finished their talk, they stood to leave the lodge and Gabe looked at Little Bull, "We will meet you on the far side of the river before first light." Little Bull glanced at Gabe, frowning, but nodded his agreement. The men parted, each going to his lodge to prepare for the coming battle. Weapons must be examined and prepared, prayers given, and loved ones embraced. Tomorrow would be a time when the mettle of each man would be tested, and some would not return, but they were determined to free the captives and chastise the captors.

29 / SETTING

Gabe rolled from his blankets just after midnight to stand before their lean-to and look up at the big moon waxing to full, the sky was clear and bedecked with stars. He stretched as he searched the skies for familiar constellations and was startled when Cougar spoke at his side, "It is a beautiful night." She tucked her hand under his arm at the crook of his elbow and he squeezed it close, as she lay her head against his shoulder she added, "Spirit Bear is restless."

"Yes I am. I felt the need to spend a little time with our Lord before the day begins, you want to join me?"

With a glance to the shelter, thinking of the little ones, she nodded and walked beside him as he climbed the ridge. The silence between them was filled with similar thoughts for each one knew what the other felt at times like this, and with hands clasped they crested the ridge. They sat down, holding each other close, and looked at the shadowed valley that was marked by the silvery ribbon of the river that twisted through the shrubbery. As their thoughts and prayers lifted to the heavens, both were laden with the probability of taking lives to save lives, but such was the way of the wilderness. Even here in the midst of God's most beautiful creation, evil touches the lives of the unsuspecting and for good to prevail, all too often the shedding of blood is required.

They walked quietly back to camp and as Gabe saddled Ebony, Cougar checked on the boys and fetched Gabe's rifle and accouterments from the shelter. She knew that Gabe's restlessness was driving him to scout out the prospector's camp. Never one to go into a fight or confrontation without thorough preparation, he had to know more about the lay of the land and the location of each of the diggings. He slipped the strap of the possibles bag over one shoulder, the powder horn over the other. Stuffed his tomahawk in his belt, felt for his knives at his back, then slipped the Ferguson rifle into the scabbard. He touched the butts of the saddle pistols, slipped his Bailes over/under into his belt, then turned to embrace Cougar.

Ezra stepped from the shadows, leading his already rigged bay, and without a word, swung aboard to wait for Gabe. Ezra glanced at Gabe knowing exactly what he was feeling. The men had been in too many battles together not to know what the other thought, and they both knew they had to know the enemy and his position better than what the Ute scouts had reported. Once mounted, the men bent down for a kiss from their women, then rode into the dim moonlight, bound for their rendezvous with evil. As they rode through the trees, Gabe was in the lead, but once at the tree line, they reined up side by side, looking into the wide valley where the Arkansa twisted its way through the tangles and snarls of the willows and berry bushes. Ezra asked quietly, "You think all them boys is bad?"

"No, after what we heard when the lieutenant was talking with that sergeant, we know they don't like what the Capitan was doing, but what they were planning for the Capitan wasn't much better."

"Too bad we can't just sit down and talk it out, you know, like grown-ups," grumbled Ezra.

Gabe chuckled, "Grown-ups huh?"

"That's what my pa used to always say, but I reckon it don't always work, especially with those like that Capitan. I have no compunction about ending his evil days!"

They rode beside the willows, listening to the whispering wind as it made the long withes dance in the moonlight. Some bullfrogs in the bogs were trying to outdo one another for the attentions of the females, a few cicadas in the sage were rattling their wings into the dark, and in the distance, coyotes sang their love songs at the stars. While Wolf padded silently before them, the shuffling of the horses' hooves sent a long-eared jackrabbit scurrying for his den. The river bent back before them, and Gabe stood in his stirrups to look at the wide alluvial plain and the gulch that scarred the flat. "Let's cross over here," he suggested, pushing Ebony through the brush to step into the giggling water. The ripples tossed the moonbeams and starlight like nymphs dancing in the darkness, wings catching the lights and casting them into the air. Gabe shook his head at the thought of such amazing examples of the wonder of God, knowing they were on a mission of death.

They crossed the narrow sagebrush flat to go to the black timber. With the thought of finding the upper diggings of the prospectors, scout out the terrain and possible cover for the attack, and then, if time, to the lower diggings for the same. Gabe glanced at the sky to estimate the time, breathed deep of the pine scented air, and nudged Ebony into the timber. They rode the edge of a draw, staying atop the slight rise of the timbered plain for about a mile and a half, and as the trees thinned, they moved further to the south, away from the lower diggings, to continue east to the smaller gulch and the upper diggings.

The smaller gulch was no more than a crooked half-mile from the bigger gulch to its headwaters where the beds of five small run-off creeks merged.

Dry now with nothing but gravel bottoms, the rocky shoulder beside a cluster of aspen showed signs of digging. Below the aspen was a stack of gear and tools, awaiting the return of the workers. Gabe and Ezra sat atop the shoulder in a slight clearing that was about two hundred feet higher than the gulch bottom. The moon shone bright upon the gravelly bottom and lanced through the thin aspen. The shadows of the pine trees stretched away from the black trees to show a jagged edged shadow along the westernmost run-off creek bottom.

Gabe leaned closer to Ezra as he pointed, "It would be easy for you and Little Bull to put men at each of those points where the trees line the creek bottoms, and you'd have the high ground and good cover, while they'd be exposed in the open."

Ezra stood in his stirrups, moving side to side to look below, then dropped into his seat, glanced at Gabe, "Looks good to me!"

"Then let's go back for another look at the lower end."

But the tree cover on the south edge of the bigger gulch was too sparse to allow them to get much of a closer look at the lower diggings and with the camp of the workers just across the gulch and in the edge of the trees on the north bank, it wasn't worth the risk. Gabe took a glance at the sky, guessed their time was short and opted for them to return to the river and await Little Bull and his men.

They heard them before they saw them, and when Gabe and Ezra stood beside the willows, they were surprised as the Ute band moved through the brush to cross the river. There were more than expected, and in the lead were the chief, shaman, war leader, and the elder, Walks on Mountains. It was a remarkable sight in the light of the almost full moon, for the leaders were arrayed in their most impressive war regalia. Stone Buffalo had an eagle feather war bonnet with a wide beaded headband, feathers each tipped with dyed horsehair, and the long, feathered bands flowed over his shoulder and down his back. With a full set of beaded and fringed buckskins, a lance that bore many scalps, the chief rode tall and proud. Beside him, Black Calf, the shaman wore his buffalo scalp headdress with horns standing tall, and white ermine tails falling at the side. He also wore beaded and fringed buckskins. Beside the shaman, Little Bull, the war leader, had a fluttery feathered headdress that had owl feathers standing like quills on a porcupine, tall and waving in the wind, his painted face with black across his forehead and white covering the rest of his face, with two thin streaks of red coming from his eyes, all doing exactly what he wanted, portraying a frightful image of impending death.

Most impressive was the tall war bonnet of Walks

on Mountains, with eagle feathers tipped with dyed tufts of rabbit fur, ermine tails that adorned the beaded headband and cascaded over the sides of his head, with the long feathered ends falling over his shoulder and trailing at the side of his mount. His buckskins were pale tan, almost white, and heavily adorned with bead and quill work. He sat tall, and even though he was but an elder and sub-chief, he exuded confidence and courage.

Ezra glanced at Gabe, "Didn't know we was supposed to dress up for this shindig!"

Gabe chuckled and swung aboard Ebony, motioned for Wolf to come close, and they waited for the chiefs to come near. As Stone Buffalo stopped before him, Gabe said, "We scouted out the camps, Ezra will tell Little Bull about the upper end, and we'll wait till they're ready before we strike, if that works for you, Stone Bull."

The chief looked from Gabe to Ezra, then motioned for Little Bull and his chosen warriors to go with Ezra. As they watched them leave, Gabe looked at Stone Bull, "It is good that you came, I am honored to be with you and Walks on Mountains." Gabe knew the Ute warriors would more readily obey the commands of their chief than him, and in a time of battle, any hesitation could be deadly.

Stone Bull nodded, then motioned for Gabe to lead the way. With a wave to Wolf, Gabe started to the trail that angled up the sharp bluff to take them to the timber and on to the lower diggings. By taking the trail through the dark timber, they would come behind the camp of the workers, but planned to wait until they had left the camp and were at work on the diggings.

30 / SKIRMISH

The grey line of early morning shaded the distant mountains into silhouettes as the band of warriors trailed behind Ezra and Little Bull. While they rode, Ezra spoke to the war leader, describing the upper end of the gulch. "There's 'bout five," holding up his hand with all fingers extended, then pointing at each finger, "little dry creeks that come together in the bottom. Each of these points," placing a finger in the notch between the fingers on the extended hand, "has good thick trees that will give cover. With a shooter at each of these points, all under good cover, we can take the workers here," pointing to his palm, "without too much trouble." He looked at the scowl on Little Bull's face and added, "But after you see it, you might have some other idea. And the plan is for us to wait for the workers, then we'll strike first."

Little Bull nodded, nudged his mount into the lead.

He believed he knew this country better than the intruders and would decide what they would do, how they would attack these takers of warriors. When they crested the slight rise above the meeting of gulches, Little Bull reined up and stepped down. The sky was showing grey, shadows stretched pointing to the west, and the gulch below held nothing but darkness. The war leader squinted, moved around some to try to see better, recognizing the points of timber told of by Ezra. Ezra stood slightly behind the war leader when Little Bull turned to look at the man. Standing behind Ezra's head was the bulky knob of his war club, the sharp edge of halberd blade, showing bright in the coming light. Bull nodded, "Do you use that in battle?"

Ezra grinned, reached to his back, and quickly drew the war club. In one smooth motion he slipped it high, caught the end with his hand and as the weight of the head brought it down, he grasped the carved handgrip in one hand and swung the club a full circle to one side, then passing it to the other hand, made a full circle on the other side. The club whistled slightly as it moved and at the completion of the second circle, Ezra grasped it with both hands and moved it in a flat slicing motion before him. Ezra grinned at the wide-eyed back-stepping Little Bull, then stood it at his side, and answered, "It is my favorite weapon!"

"But you have the guns of the white man," stated Little Bull as if asking a question.

"Ummhmm, and I use them, but close-up, this is best," nodding to the war club. He hefted it before him, then handed it to Little Bull to examine.

The war leader was surprised at the weight of the iron wood war club but was pleased with the balance and ease of handling as he swung it side to side. Ezra watched, but caught movement at the corner of his eye, held up his hand, "We got comp'ny!" he spoke softly. Both men dropped into a crouch and looked to the gulch below. Ezra stepped back, cupped his hands, and gave the call of the night hawk in the direction of the others.

Gabe motioned for the others to stay and with a nod to Stone Bull, started to the edge of the trees. The sun was starting to bend its golden swords over the eastern mountains, stretching the shadows toward the valley when Gabe and Stone Buffalo stepped down and went stealthily to the edge of the bluff. Below them, the camp was full of activity as they prepared for another day at the gold diggings. The captives had been bound together and lashed to a pair of tree stumps that remained from a long-ago fire. The Capitan was barking orders as two men worked at the captives' bonds, releasing them from the stumps but leaving them bound together. Another man passed out strips of smoked meat to the captives, their only food for the day of work ahead.

The degraded Ute eagerly accepted the meat, some chewing on the ration immediately, others stuffing it in their breechcloth for later.

The Capitan stomped through the camp, gesturing, and shouting at the men, anxious to get to the upper gulch and what he hoped would be an even greater deposit of gold. Diego stepped forward, "How many Indians do you want to take with you?"

The Capitan stopped, scowled at Diego, "Dos, and three men. We will ride, and they," spitting at the natives, "will walk! Or we'll drag them behind!"

Diego lifted one eyebrow, dropping his gaze from the Capitan, mumbled, "Si, Capitan," and turned away to do his bidding. Within moments, the Capitan and his group rode from the camp, and it was but a few moments later when Gabe heard the distant scream of the nighthawk. He knew the upper diggings were no more than a half mile away, a distance covered in moments by a horse. He grinned and looked at Stone Buffalo, "Little Bull and his men are ready."

Stone Buffalo frowned, then remembered the nighthawk, and nodded in that direction, "Your friend?"

Gabe nodded, then pointed to both ends of the bluff above the camp below, "Do you want to come from there," turning to point to the south of the bluff, "And I'll come from there?" The chief looked where Gabe pointed, and nodded his agreement. Gabe added, "When we hear Little Bull's attack, then we move. I'll follow your lead."

"It is good," answered Stone Buffalo, turning back to his mount. Once aboard, he turned to motion his men, and with a wave of his hand, divided the remaining warriors, one group to follow him, the others to follow Gabe. He nudged his mount into the trees, turning to move further up the edge of the butte to the chosen point of descent. Gabe waved to the others to follow him, surprised to see Walks on Mountains choose to go with him.

Stone Buffalo took the trail from the butte that cut through a thicket of aspen, leaving enough cover so they could descend the butte unseen. The chief had the shaman and eight warriors, Gabe had Walks on Mountains and seven warriors. The chief was in position before Gabe, but the trail followed by the band dropped them from the butte just behind a stand of cottonwood that sided the small creek. They were in a slight depression and shielded from view by the workers when Gabe turned to Walks on Mountains, "Do you want to lead this charge?"

The old man grinned, looking at Gabe with a smile, then slowly nodded, "It will be good."

Little Bull returned Ezra's war club and swung aboard his mount. He had already sent men to each point and they would be awaiting his order to begin the assault. With a glance to Ezra, he pushed his mount through the trees to come into the gulch behind the workers and captives. Ezra knew Gabe and the others would be waiting for the sound of gunfire before they started their attack, so he slipped his Lancaster from the sheath beneath his right leg and lay it across the pommel. He checked the pan and frizzen, and satisfied, followed Little Bull from the trees to drop into the dry creek bed of the narrow gulch. The captives were on long tethers as they walked behind the mounted riders and quickly turned when they heard horses behind them. The uplifted hand of Little Bull silenced them, and they continued to walk behind the mounted workers.

When the Capitan reached the head of the gulch, he drew his mount to a stop and swung his leg over the animal's rump, but his eyes were on the rocky edge of the small bluff, the spot he was certain held a great vein of gold. The other workers had started to dismount when Little Bull let loose his war cry and Ezra dropped the hammer on the Lancaster. His target was the Capitan, but just as Little Bull screamed, the Capitan's horse bolted, and Ezra's bullet tore a trench across the seat of the Capitan's saddle, narrowly missing the Capitan's head.

Ezra slipped his Lancaster back into the sheath, grabbed his war club and drove his heels into the ribs of his big bay. The horse lunged forward, barely missing one of the captives, and Ezra drove him into the horse of the nearest worker, pushing him against the man and the horse beside him. Ezra made a swooping swing with his warclub and sliced open the top of the workers head, just before he could pull the trigger on the rifle aimed at Ezra's chest. The horses of the workers bolted, clamoring against one another and the workers that fought to get their rifles or pistols in use. An arrow whispered past Ezra and buried itself in the neck of one of the men. Another rifle barked and a warrior fell into the gulch, blood blossoming at his chest.

Ezra saw the Capitan trying to climb the steep rocks at the head of the gulch, and slapped legs to the bay, charging after the man. As the bay drove his front feet into the sandy bottom to slide to a stop, Ezra was already coming off. He lunged to the bottom of the rocks, saw the man above him lift his pistol, and Ezra dropped to his knee against the stony face of the abutment. The pistol fired and the bullet whiffed past his head, as Ezra grinned and stepped away from the rocks. He hollered to the Capitan as his footing was slipping on the loose rock, "Oh Capitan! O Capitan!" sounding like a woman calling her husband to dinner. He paused, chuckling, "I have a pistol aimed at your rear! If you want me to shoot you where you can't sit down, or perhaps I'll miss and shoot you in the back, I will be happy to oblige. But if you want to live, you will turn around and come down!"

The Capitan had stopped moving, trying to look down at the man who was speaking, then twisted around, saw Ezra, and frowned. "You are a black man!" he declared. "What are you doing with these heathen?"

"Come on down and I will explain it to you Capitan!" retorted a grinning Ezra. The Capitan replaced his pistol in his bandolier, felt the second pistol and smiled to himself as he thought, *How foolish this man is, no wonder they are all slaves.* He called down, "I will come down, but the footing is bad. It will take some doing."

"We're in no hurry, Capitan. We will wait for you!" Ezra replied, and stuffed his pistol in his belt as he brought his war club around. He lay the weapon on his shoulder, knowing the man was going to try something, because a man like this does not give himself up so easily. Ezra fingered the war club, lifting it slightly off his shoulder as he watched the man feeling for a place for his foot as he began his descent. Ezra watched his hands, both above his head and clinging to the rocks, until he moved his foot more and dropped his right hand to his side, out of Ezra's line of sight. Ezra thought, *Here it comes!* and lifted the warclub, rocking back with it behind him. As the Capitan started to turn, Ezra let the club fly. It made the sound of the beating wings of an eagle as it tumbled end over end with the weighted end and the halberd blade coming upright just as it neared the man on the ledge. As the muzzle of the pistol appeared at the Capitan's side, the halberd blade was buried in the back of the man's head, splitting his skull and splattering detritus over the rocky face of the butte.

The low thunder of gunfire rolled over the flat, and chief Stone Buffalo lifted his arm, looked to either side at his men, then shouted his war cry and kicked his horse to charge. The big paint lunged forward, crashing through the brush, warriors on either side but slightly behind, each screaming their war cries, waving lances in the air, others with arrows nocked on their bows, each one splitting the morning with their screams.

The workers were startled and momentarily frozen in fear until Diego shouted, "Get your rifles!" Every worker had been ordered to keep their rifles near and they dove for their weapons. Arrows thudded into the rocker boxes that some hid behind, the clatter of hooves over the rocky banks of the creek added to the pandemonium. Two workers lifted their rifles and fired at the charging horde, but one of the captives lifted his shovel overhead and smashed it down on the skull of the shooter. When the man crumpled to the ground, the captive warrior screamed his war cry and chopped at the man's neck with the blade of the shovel. Blood poured from the mangled neck, covering the gold rich gravel with a dark red that dimmed the lure of gold. Other workers grabbed their weapons only to be skewered with lances driven by angered warriors atop charging war horses.

Diego shouted to Sergeant Alvares, "Your pistol, use your pistol!" as the man was frantically trying to reload the rifle in his hands. The sergeant looked up, saw Diego motioning to the side, making Alvares turn as he snatched the pistol from his belt. He lifted the weapon, earring back the hammer and pulled the trigger, more as a reaction to the arrow driving into his chest, than by his aim, but the bullet flew true and unseated a charging Ute, a young warrior that fell to the side as his horse lunged from the bank of the creek.

Gabe was close beside Walks on Mountains as the chief lay along his horse's neck, charging into the battle. He held his lance low, choosing his target through the flying mane and guided his mount with his knees as he neared Lieutenant Gomez. The Spaniard turned at the sound of hoofbeats, lifting his pistol and bringing it to full cock. He stood his ground, taking aim at the feathered warrior, but as he started to squeeze the trigger, a monstrous black stallion drove him to the ground, smashing his face with massive hooves, kicking gravel and dirt over him as he thundered past. Diego groaned, rolled to the side, put a hand to his jaw and felt it out of place. His eyes closed as he felt blood coming from his mouth and nose. He tried to rise, but the flint point of a lance drove into his back and pinned him to the ground.

Gabe had drawn one of the saddle pistols, eared back one hammer, and watched the melee before him. Stone Buffalo had run a worker through with his lance, pulled it free and looked for another target. Gabe saw one of the workers lift his rifle to take aim on the chief, then dug heels into Ebony to charge. As the man readied his aim, Gabe fired. The pistol bucked and the bullet found its mark in the man's shoulder, knocking him sideways, dropping him to the ground. Gabe brought Ebony to sliding stop, earing back the second hammer as he did, looked down at the man who was digging at his belt for his pistol when Gabe spoke in Spanish, "*No dispares*!"

The man frowned at Gabe, "You are a white man!"

Gabe nodded, still holding the pistol toward the man, but the man still drew his own pistol as he said, "You shot that already!" The worker grinned as he lifted his pistol, but before Gabe could pull the trigger, Wolf lunged and drove the man to his back, tearing at his throat and muffling the man's screams. Another worker ran to help his friend, lifted his pistol to shoot the beast ripping at the man on the ground, but Gabe dropped the hammer on the second barrel and the pistol spat death to the stubborn worker. Gabe jammed the pistol in the holster, drew the second one, cocking the hammer as he did. Looking around for another target, he nudged Ebony close to where Walks on Mountain sat, watching the battle subside. It had only been a few moments, but the Ute overwhelmed the workers, and several were already among the dead, taking their trophies. Gabe saw several of the captives, easily discerned for they wore only breech-cloths, having been stripped of their breeches by the Spaniards, as they moved among the bodies of the workers, spitting on them, and mutilating the bodies.

Gabe saw three workers, bound together as were the captives, seated near one of the sluices and watched over by Black Calf, the shaman. He turned to Walks on Mountains, "What will happen to them?" nodding toward the bound workers.

Walks shook his head, "They will be taken back to the village. The women who lost their men will have their way with them. Some might be made slaves, but I think these will not."

31 / WIDOWS

It was a joyful time when the returning warriors rode into the village, rescued warriors riding on the captured horses taken from the Spaniards. The many mules trailed along behind, mixing with the herded horses, but the Ute were uncertain about the strange long-eared animals. Although they had seen mules before, some of the Spanish and French traders used them as pack animals, they were different enough that the Ute were somewhat wary. But the presence of the mules did little to hamper the rejoicing and mood of celebration, however there were some lodges where wailing and mourning was heard. This was the first time the women knew who had lost a man among those killed when the others were captured and those that had died in the recent battle.

When the band of warriors rode into the village, the captured Spaniards were led with rawhide braided tethers around their necks, their hands tied behind their backs. They stumbled along behind the warriors who rode, each one a freed captive, enjoying the vengeance of leading their captors. Stone Buffalo stepped down before his lodge, turned and ordered the captives to be bound and spread-eagled to stakes in the ground. He lifted his hands high for the people to listen, "We have had a great victory and your men are returned. Some have crossed over and the women of those warriors will have say about these," pointing to the captives as they were forced to the ground to be bound. "These," he spat as he spoke, "have caused the death of many of our brave warriors, some of our men were whipped and beaten as they were bound and forced to work at that which was not meant for man, to dig in the dirt like a badger!" Many of the people shouted, some screamed, and the wailing of the widows rose like a tide of mourning and covered the village.

Gabe and Ezra had ridden with the chief and leaders as they came into the village but started to turn away and leave until Stone Buffalo stopped them. He lifted his hands again, "These men," nodding to Gabe and Ezra, "Spirit Bear and Black Buffalo, have proven themselves friends of the Mouache and are to be treated with great honor!" The screams of anger turned into shouts of joy and thankfulness as many of the villagers crowded around the two, though wary of Wolf who stood beside Gabe, and touched them and thanked them.

A short while later the people had dispersed, preparing for a celebratory feast and dance, and Gabe and Ezra returned to their camp. The women heard their approach and stood, looking through the trees for a glimpse and reassurance that both of their men were returning. At first sight, they broke into a run and greeted their men at the edge of the trees before they could dismount. As they walked beside them into the camp, Wolf trotted before them, anxious to play with the children.

With the horses stripped of their gear, rubbed down, and tethered on the grass, Gabe and Ezra walked quietly back to the fire. The women happily poured their men a cup of coffee which was more chicory than coffee and sat beside them. It was a few moments of silence to savor the return of the men and rescue of the captives. As Gabe sat, elbow on knees, cup cradled in his hands, and staring into the low flames, Cougar asked, "Was it bad?"

"Not like sometimes in the past. All the prospectors were killed but three. They were brought to the village and Walks on Mountains said the widows will have their way with them."

Cougar said, "It is the way of the people."

"What do you think will be done to 'em?" asked Ezra, glancing from Cougar to Dove.

"There are more women that lost their men than those that have been taken. Some women want to strike back and destroy those that took their men. Others will grieve and need a man to provide for them and will choose to make the captive a slave, and sometimes the captive becomes a part of the people and becomes the man of the lodge. When there are so many that grieve and are angry, and so few that are captives, their punishment will be great." Dove dropped her eyes to the ground, remembering times she had witnessed similar things in her village.

"Grief is a hard thing. It blinds the one grieving and the anger within drives them to do that which is not the usual way of the person," added Cougar.

"Ummhmm," drawled Gabe, eyes glazed as he looked at the fire, "we saw a lot of that today." He was remembering the images of the warriors scalping and mutilating the bodies of the Spaniards, crazed in their drive for vengeance, they cut and chopped at the bodies until none would be recognizable. He shook his head to clear his mind of the images, glanced at Ezra, "Did the Capitan fall?"

Ezra just nodded, saying nothing but remembering the image of the man's head splitting and blood splattering the rockface. There was a morbid satisfaction in the man's death, but a haunting memory of the way he died at Ezra's hand.

Their moment of reverie was interrupted by the

sound of horse's hooves on the trail from the village. Gabe stood, hand naturally dropping to the pistol in his belt, looking through the trees to see two horses coming up the trail. He glanced to Ezra who stood and stepped away from the fire, standing apart from Gabe and looking at the trail. The first of the riders was the familiar figure of Hawk that Screams, the son of chief Stone Buffalo, but the second horse carried a woman, head hanging with her hands twisted in the mane of her mount that was led by Hawk. They came to the edge of the camp and stopped, Hawk looked at the men, lifted his head to look at the women, and asked, "This is the mother of my friend Spotted Deer. She needs help and our village has too many women that are grieving. I thought perhaps," as he looked down to see Cougar come alongside Gabe, and nodded toward her, "your women could help."

Cougar and Dove stepped close to the woman, helped her slide to the ground. One braid had been cut off, her buckskin tunic was torn and bloody, and both arms were covered with blood. The women helped her to their shelter, lay her on the blankets and began tending to her wounds, softly speaking as they worked, trying to reassure the grieving woman.

Gabe and Ezra led Hawk that Screams to the fire, motioned for him to be seated as they sat down opposite the young man. They waited for Hawk to speak, giving him time to form his words. He breathed deep and began, "My friend, the one you saw with me in the woods when we met, was with us at the battle. He was killed by the bullet of one of the workers before my arrow took him down. This was his first battle, and he fought bravely."

Both Gabe and Ezra noticed Hawk did not use his friend's name, understanding the way of some tribes as they believed the using of a man's name after his death was to call the evil side of the departed spirit to return.

Hawk added, "His father, Singing Bird's man, was one of the first to die when our warriors were taken. She grieves her man and her son."

"Does she have any other family?" asked Gabe.

"No. Little Bird was taken by our people in a raid on a village of the Arapaho when she was but a small child. She has been a part of our village since that time. The family that took her as their own, crossed over many summers past."

"What will happen to her?" asked Ezra.

"She is the mother of my friend. I will do what I can to help her, our village always watches over the women of lost warriors. Now there are more women than men and for her to find a man of her own . . ." he shrugged.

Cougar came from the shelter to stand beside Gabe, looked at Hawk that Screams, "Singing Bird is quiet now. It would be good if she stayed with us so we can help her at this time."

"Will she be alright?" asked Hawk, standing as he spoke to Cougar.

"Yes, it will take time, but she must grieve and begin to look ahead. We can help her during this time."

"When should I return for her?"

Cougar smiled, "When she is ready, we will bring her back to the village."

Hawk smiled, nodding, "It is good. She has lost both her men; it will be hard for her."

Cougar frowned, "Both her men?"

"Yes, my friend who came with me to your camp, was her son, he was killed in the battle today. Her man was one of those killed when the others were taken captive." Cougar frowned, nodding, and glanced back to the shelter where Dove sat with the grieving woman.

Hawk looked at Gabe, "I must return to my village. My father asked for you and your family to join us for the feast at the end of this day. Will you come?"

"Perhaps," answered Gabe, standing. He looked from Hawk to Cougar and back, then added, "Probably." Hawk grinned and went to his horse, swung aboard, and left to return to the village.

Gabe looked at Cougar, "I was surprised he brought her here until he told us she had no other family. With so many grieving, she had no one to turn to for help."

"It is good that Hawk brought her here. We will

take care of her and maybe give her help that the others in the village could not give."

Gabe frowned at his woman who smiled as she turned away, then glanced at Ezra. "You know, I think they learn that at a very early age."

Ezra frowned, "What?"

"The way they do that, say something that tells you nothing but raises your curiosity and then smile and walk away, leaving you to wonder just what they were talking about or what they're up to! Frustrating, that's what it is, frustrating!"

"Yeah, but we love 'em for it!" answered a grinning Ezra.

32 / SOLACE

The feast was less of a celebration than Gabe and Ezra had expected. The mourning of the families hung like a pall over the village and the dances took on more of a manner of grieving for the dead than a celebration for the return of the living. They sat opposite Stone Buffalo and Little Bull when the chief spoke, "Our men have taken many weapons from the dead, but they do not know how they are used," he paused as he looked from Gabe to Ezra, "You have these same weapons and they bring death from the hands of one who knows these weapons. It would be good for our warriors to know about them."

Gabe ate while he listened to the chief, waited for the chief to say more, but he sat watching Gabe, expecting an answer to the unasked question. Gabe wiped his greasy hands on the legs of his buckskins, looked from Little Bull to Stone Buffalo, "Does the chief of the mighty Mouache Ute people ask me and my brother to teach the warriors about these weapons?"

"Are these weapons good for hunting buffalo?"

"Yes, they can be very useful in the hands of a warrior that knows the weapons."

Stone Buffalo reached behind his blanket and brought out two leather pouches, obviously heavy, and sat them before him. He motioned to them, "This is what those men were digging for in the stream, what they killed our warriors for and made them dig. It is yours if you will teach my warriors about these weapons."

Gabe answered, "That," nodding to the pouches, "is of no use for us, but we," glancing to Ezra, "will show your warriors about these weapons because we are friends of the Ute people."

Stone Buffalo let a slight smile tug at the corners of his mouth but dropped his eyes to the pouches and pushed them closer to Gabe as he said, "It is good." He looked at Little Bull and nodded.

The war leader leaned slightly forward as he began, "Our people mourn those that have crossed over. There are many lodges that are empty because of those," nodding toward the far side of the valley where the battle occurred, "these must be prepared for burial and their things and more will be with them. It is the wish of our people that you and your families stay with our people for a season or as long as you wish. We would be honored for you to be a part of our village."

Gabe was surprised by the invitation, especially voiced by Little Bull, the man that had shown no liking for their presence. He glanced at Ezra and back to Little Bull and to Stone Buffalo. He started to answer, but Stone Buffalo held up a hand to stop him and began, "We lost many of our warriors and our village has been made weak. Before the season of colors, we will go south for our buffalo hunt, and then to our encampment by the springs of hot water for the cold season. The custom of our people when a warrior crosses over is to bury him with his weapons so he may hunt on the other side and defend his family also. Many of his things are buried with him, but the lodge of his family is empty. We offer two of these lodges for your families."

Gabe dropped his eyes to the ground, thinking for a moment, then looked at the chief, "We are honored by all that you have said," glancing to Little Bull to include him in the comments, "and we will give much thought to these things. We were traveling to the south to learn of this great land and the people of these mountains." He paused a moment, then added, "We," pointing to Ezra with his chin, "will talk of these things and decide. We will speak again tomorrow."

Cougar sat by the fire, the Bible on her lap, as she read a favorite passage from the book of Psalms. She smiled as she read, prompting Dove to ask, "What gives you joy this morning, sister?" The women were alone with the children and Singing Bird while Gabe and Ezra had gone hunting.

Cougar smiled as she looked up to answer Dove, pointed to the pages of the Bible and answered, "This part that says, *'He shall cover thee with his feathers, and under his wings shall thou trust: his truth shall be thy shield and buckler. Thou shalt not be afraid for the terror by night; nor for the arrow that flieth by day.'"* She looked up at Dove, "It makes me think of the eagles I have seen in their nest. If a storm comes, the eagle will spread his wings over the nest to protect the young." She paused, looking down at the pages and back to Dove, "That's how God is with us!"

Dove smiled, nodding, and glanced to see Singing Bird frowning as she watched Cougar and Dove. With a slight nod toward Singing Bird, Dove directed Cougar's attention to the woman. When Cougar saw the expression of concern on her face, she asked, "Singing Bird, is something wrong?"

Bird pointed to the book on Cougar's lap, "What is that?"

Cougar smiled as she lifted the Bible to show their visitor, "This is a Bible. It has the words of God written down for us to read."

Bird frowned, not understanding, and moved closer to see the pages. She reached out to touch the page, felt its smoothness, but frowned at the markings. She looked up at Cougar, wonder showing in her eyes and Cougar smiled as she began to explain, "Our people make signs on rocks that tell of things that happened long ago. You have seen them?"

Bird smiled, "Yes, there are some on the cliffs near the river," she responded enthusiastically. "They tell of a long-ago battle with the Crow. And others tell of hunts for buffalo and other animals, strange animals like I have never seen."

Cougar continued, "These," pointing to the pages, "are like those images on the cliffs and tell of things of long ago and more." She paused, letting Bird comprehend what was said, then continued, "The words I just read about the wings like the eagle is like a picture on the rocks that tell of the love of God."

Bird frowned, "This God, is that the same as what we call *Senawahv*, the Creator?"

Cougar dropped her gaze for a moment of thought, "Do you believe that *Senawahv* created all things and has power over all things?"

"I think so, but it is the shaman that speaks for and prays to *Senawahv*. We ask the other gods of the animals, like the coyote, and the forests and rocks, and others to give us what we need."

Cougar nodded slowly, took a deep breath, "The God that I know, we believe is the only God. He tells us here," pointing to the Bible, "about how He created the world and all the animals, mountains, and us. And He also watches over us, talks to us through His Word," tapping the pages, "and we are to pray to Him for what we need." She looked at Bird and continued, "When we hurt, He gives comfort, and when we are afraid, He protects us, like the eagle in the nest."

Bird looked up, smiling, and asked, "Can I know this God?"

Cougar smiled, "Yes, because He says many times how He loves us and wants us to know Him." She paused, and added, "You are like I was before I knew this God," her hand lay on the Bible as Bird looked down, "and my man told me how easy it is to know Him." She flipped the pages of the Bible to the book of Romans and said, "Let me tell you . . ." she began as she told of the words in the pages, pointing to them even though she knew Bird could not read them, and explained about the four things that God wants her to know.

"First, is that we are all sinners, what that means is there have been times when what we do or think or say are not good things. Maybe it was when you hurt someone with your words or did something you know was bad. That is called sin, and we have all done bad things. Do you understand?"

As Bird nodded, Cougar continued, "Next, we need to know that because we've done bad things, what we get for that is punished, like when you punish your child for doing wrong, but what we should get is death."

"But everyone dies," protested Bird, frowning.

"Yes, and since we did wrong, when we die, we deserve to burn forever in a terrible place called Hell."

Bird flinched at the words, frowning and pulling back, but Cougar gently put her hand on Bird's arm and continued, "But this verse," pointing to Romans 5:8, "says God showed His love to us and sent his son to die for us."

"You mean He sent his own son to die for us so we wouldn't have to die?"

Cougar smiled, nodding, "So we would not have to go to that place called Hell. His son, Jesus, came and died to pay for a gift, a very special gift, the gift of eternal life."

"What is . . . eternal life?"

"Instead of going to that place called Hell, we can go to Heaven," pointing to the sky, "where God lives, and live forever with Him, never dying."

"That is a gift? But what do we have to give Him for that gift?" Cougar knew she was thinking of the custom of her people that if one receives a gift, they must give a gift of equal or greater value in return.

Cougar smiled, touching Bird's arm again, "We do

not have to give anything in return. All we have to do is ask for that gift in prayer."

Bird sat still, thinking, and unmoving for several moments. She looked at the Bible on Cougar's lap, lifted her eyes to Cougar, "If I do this, will I understand those tracks?" pointing with her chin to the Bible.

Cougar paused, "If you do this, knowing here," putting her hand to her heart to emphasize her words, "that it is the right thing to do and you want it with all you know, you will understand these words." She paused, and explained, "But you will not be able to read them until you learn the language of the white man and learn how to read the tracks like you read the sign on a trail."

"Will you teach me?" asked Bird, glancing from Cougar to Dove who was watching over the rambunctious children.

"I do not know how long we will be here, Bird. If our men decide to leave, then we must go, but while we are here, I will try to teach you. It takes many moons of teaching and learning to know these things."

"I will ponder what you have said. I think this is what I needed to know, about a God that loves and watches over His people and makes the trail for us to cross over and be with Him. It is good, I will think on this."

Cougar reached out to pull Bird close and hug her.

When they sat back, tears showed in Bird's eyes, and when she looked at Cougar, she smiled, "I do not shed tears for grief, but for friends." She nodded to Dove and looked back at Cougar, "You are my friends."

"Then let friends prepare the meal for our men, they will soon return and will be ready to eat!" declared Dove, coming near the two that sat on the log. She glanced back at the children, the older boys playing with Wolf and the younger ones rolling on the blankets, chasing the drumming tail of Wolf.

Cougar glanced to the sky, saw it was nearing midday and joined Dove in the preparing of the timpsila. They ground the dried roots into a flour and added it to the pot of boiling fresh timpsila root slices, potatoes, and onions to make a thick gravy, once the men returned with the fresh meat. Bird began mixing a batter for cornpone cakes while Dove added some grounds to the coffee pot. They chattered all the while, talking of children, seasons, and men. But when they heard the approach of the hunters, Dove and Cougar looked through the trees for the first sight of their men, anxiously smiling and anticipating their return.

When the meal was finished, the pots and platters cleaned, and the men sat back to enjoy their coffee, Singing Bird looked to Cougar and asked, "Will you show me how to receive that gift?" Cougar smiled, glanced at Gabe, and walked away with Bird for their quiet time of prayer. They sat on a large flat boulder that lay near the trees and offered an overlook of the lake, the waters placid and the reflection of the mountains showing as a mirror image on the surface.

Cougar took Bird's hand in hers and said, "The gift you seek is offered freely by our God, but it was purchased by the sacrifice of His Son when he died on the cross to pay for our sins. It is like any other gift and will not be ours until we accept it." She looked at Bird who watched with expectant eyes and nodded.

"I will pray, and as I pray, if you truly want this gift, and if you mean it here," she put her hand over her heart and wrinkled her forehead as she looked at Bird, "then repeat the words as I say." Bird nodded and Cougar began, "Our Father in Heaven, . . ." and continued by asking forgiveness for sin, and simply asked for the gift of eternal life. Bird clearly repeated the words, but her voice choked slightly causing Cougar to look up to see tears coursing down Bird's cheeks, but she finished repeating the words, and Cougar finished the prayer with an *Amen!*

The women embraced one another, laughed, and cried together, and rose to return to the camp.

33 / SEASONS

"What are we gonna do with those pouches," bewailed Ezra, looking at Gabe and shaking his head as they sat opposite one another, the cookfire between them.

"You mean those pouches with the gold?" asked Gabe.

"What other pouches you think I'd be talkin' about, of course those pouches! It ain't like we got any use for the stuff, it's not like we can put on our fancy duds and climb in the carriage and go to the market and spend it!"

"I was thinkin' about that, and I figger we'd just melt it down, and put it in the bottom of our saddle bags and forget about it, but keep it on the off chance we might one day be somewhere it can be used."

Ezra frowned, "And where might that somewhere be? And when might that one day be?"

Gabe chuckled, watched Cougar come from

the hide lodge, the boys following close behind, "I dunno. We're goin' south and if we were to one day keep goin', we might eventually end up in Santa Fe. Or maybe one day our boys might want to go see what civilization is all about and it would come in handy in the city."

"So, you say we should just pack around all that gold just in case our kids grow up and wanna go to town!"

"Well, when you put it that way . . ." he laughed as he leaned forward to refill his cup with the chicory/coffee blend. He smiled as he thought, "It would buy us enough coffee to last a while."

Ezra shook his head, adding to his cup, when Dove put her hand on his back and said, "You two great hunters will watch Fox and Squirrel while we go gather roots and more for our meals."

Ezra turned to look at Dove, frowning as Squirrel lifted her arms to her daddy to lift her to his lap. He glanced to Gabe who had Fox sitting beside him, twisting the fringe on his britches in his fingers. "You notice, that was not a request, just a statement. 'You will watch . . .' she said, and there they go, pretty as you please, leavin' us with diaper duty!"

Gabe chuckled as he looked at the little ones, then looked at Ezra, "Stone Buffalo said they were considering moving south soon. The buffalo like the valley of this river," nodding to the Arkansa in the bottom of the valley, "further south. He said it widens out and has ample grass for them to hang out most of the summer before they migrate to the warm country."

"I been gettin' a hankerin' for some good buffalo steak," declared Ezra. He chuckled for a moment, then added, "After what we taught them fellas 'bout those muskets, they're prob'ly thinkin' killin' a big buff's gonna be easy! Just wait'll they find out how mad one 'o them big bulls get when they get a bullet under their hides!" he laughed at the image, shaking his head.

"Ummhmmm, it's hard to make 'em realize that the white man's rifle isn't all they think it is, but they'll find out soon enough."

They were silent for a while, sipping their coffee and pondering life as they stared at the low-burning flames of the fire. Ezra looked up and asked, "So, you thinkin' 'bout stayin' with the Ute through the winter?"

"Dunno. The lodges are great, but not the same as a cozy cabin, especially in the harsh snowstorms of the mountains."

"Little Bull says those hot springs where they have their winter camp are good bathing and also make it warmer in the valley where they camp," surmised Ezra.

"Guess we'll just wait 'n see," answered Gabe. "We can always build a cabin if we prefer."

"Only if we get started on it soon enough. I ain't too fond of tryin' to cut logs and build a cabin in the middle of winter."

It was late morning of the second day when Gabe and Ezra broke from the narrow valley of the river into to wider valley that lay below the towering mountains on the west. The river moved closer to the rolling foothills on the east and the big peaks of the Sawatch range seemed to tuck themselves behind the near timber covered foothills. The flatlands were pocked with sage that stood above the bunch grass and buffalo grass, scraggly cholla blossomed with yellow and bright pink blossoms above the prickly branches, the hillsides clung to random piñon and juniper. Nearer the river, the wide banks were heavy with greenery, tall grasses, berry bushes, and cottonwood that shaded the thick willows.

Hawk that Screams pointed to the long slopes and dark shoulder that flanked the higher mountains, "Our winter camp is below those mountains. The valley with white rocks has the hot springs where we camp."

"How far?" asked Ezra as the three scouts followed the wide trail to climb the shoulder of the long flat. When they crested the rise, Gabe reined up to take in the vista of the long line of narrow tipped peaks.

"One more day," answered Hawk that Screams.

Although Dove and Cougar were with the villagers and trailed the packhorses with travois and the hide lodges, Gabe had the big grey running free rein behind

Ebony and Ezra had the mule on a long lead. They had been recruited by Hawk that Screams to scout ahead as several other young warriors were scouting in other directions. Not only were they scouting but they were also hunting meat for the village.

Hawk pointed before them, "There is a stream there. It is where we will camp for the night. It is also a good place for elk."

The trail rounded the point of trees that came from the foothills and the stream showed like a dark line across the dry flats. As the trail turned west into the mouth of the valley, Gabe pulled Ebony to a stop, stood in his stirrups, then turned to Ezra and Hawk, "There's a big herd of elk grazing just this side of that stream."

The eager Hawk nudged his mount beside Ebony and shaded his eyes as he searched the distant flats. He grinned as he recognized the dark forms less than a mile distant, turned to Gabe, "Our people need the meat!"

Gabe grinned, motioned to the sheathed musket Hawk had under his leg and said, "How 'bout you and Ezra goin' out there and getting a couple, then."

Ezra handed the lead of the mule to Gabe and motioned to Hawk to join him and turned the bay to the edge of the trees and start for the herd. The many finger ridges that skirted the foothills held the dark trees, but the tree line ended at the point of each ridge, making it difficult to approach the herd unnoticed. Ezra spoke quietly to Hawk, pointing with his chin as he spoke, "We'll work around the point yonder, that way we'll keep the herd from breaking into the valley. When threatened, they usually head for high country or thick timber and we'll be there waiting for 'em."

Within moments, the two hunters had reached the steep embankment of the stream, tethered their horses, and started back closer to the herd. Ezra led the way, and the closer they moved to the herd, the slower their stalk. Ezra dropped to one knee beside a tall sage, spoke quietly to Hawk, "You take the first shot. Take your time and squeeze it off."

Hawk grinned, moved to the far side of the sage and took a knee, slowly lifted his musket, and steadied his aim. He breathed deep, let a little out and slowly squeezed the trigger. The musket roared, kicked against Hawk's shoulder as it bucked, and belched a cloud of smoke. Ezra hesitated a moment, watching Hawk's target stumble, and moved his sights to his own young bull. The confused herd milled about, but Ezra squeezed off his shot before they spooked, but the blast from his Lancaster rifle caused the entire herd to move as if they were connected to one another. They crashed across the stream, stampeding through the willows and alders, moving like a brown and tan blanket to swing back to the mouth of the valley and run into the thick timber, leaving a thin dust cloud in their wake.

Hawk stood, trotted to the side of the downed bull, and poked it with the muzzle of his rifle, but the animal was dead. He shouted as he lifted his rifle into the air, excited about his first elk kill. He had downed deer and antelope with his bow, but this was his first elk, and he was proud. Ezra's bull was also down, and he called to Hawk, "Now begins the hard work!"

34 / CHALK

Gabe rode beside Cougar, Bobcat sitting behind the cantle of his saddle, his hands in Gabe's belt as he craned from side to side to take in the countryside, always searching for Wolf and any other animals that might be found on the sagebrush flats. Fox sat between Cougar and the pommel of her saddle, strapped to his mother with a modified harness often used for a cradle board but now made useful for the boy that was always on the move. The long-legged appaloosa colt bounded along beside his mother with Cougar and Fox aboard. Gabe looked at Cougar and his youngest son, smiled, and said a quick silent prayer of thanksgiving for his family. Cougar led the steeldust mustang trailing the travois, and the big grey was following Ebony as if they were best of friends. Ezra and his family followed close behind, also with the pack animals on leads and children on the saddles.

It was a typical day in the mountains, pristine blue sky, cool breeze that whisper from the granite tipped peaks that raised their silvery grey heads above timberline to stand as pillars supporting the arching blue canopy. Snowpack still lingered in the shaded high-up gulches, flashing white against the dark timber that draped over the steep slopes like a silken cape. The grey and tan shades of the flats lay low in contrast to the sculpted peaks, and the wide trail pointed like a dusty arrow to their destination.

Stone Buffalo led the long line nearer the foothills, shadowing the dark tree line, and came to a stop on the brink of the flat mesa that stood above the green valley, ripe with aspen, willows, and cottonwood. The silvery ribbon of an unspoiled stream danced through the valley bottom, sending bright arrows of reflected sunshine toward the travelers. As Gabe came beside Stone Buffalo, Cougar beside him, they looked past their right shoulder at a dazzling white cliff face at the steep edge of the towering mountain. Below the jagged cliffs stretched a wide alluvial plain, dotted with juniper and piñon that contrasted the deep green of the conifers with the white of the washed down rock and soil. The chalk like cliffs stood whiter than spring snow, the brilliance marred only by the few tenacious piñon that found footing on the lesser slopes. In the bottom of the valley, the plain had pushed the resilient stream to the far side of the canyon, but the waterway carved its way through to carry its life sustaining water to the herds of the flatlands.

Gabe leaned forward and frowned as he looked below at a turquoise gem that lay near the stream bed. He glanced at Stone Buffalo and the chief answered, "The hot springs. In the cold season, the steam rises, and it is hard to see the water, but now, it is good."

Gabe looked around the valley below, scanned the lower end of the hills nearby, and noticed other small pools and asked, "Are those hot springs also?"

Stone Buffalo nodded, "Yes. There are many. It is good to have others so everyone can use them. But some are too hot and must be avoided."

"I understand," answered Gabe, remembering the many hot springs in the area of the summer encampment of the Shoshone and others nearby.

Stone Buffalo looked at Gabe, then pointed to the area directly below the mesa, and the flats above the creek on the far side. "We will make our camp here, and there," pointing to the shoulder above the creek. Gabe looked at the far flat, saw the timbered bluffs that fronted the flat and the ample timber, and began considering as he surveyed the valley.

When Stone Buffalo nudged his mount to the trail that angled off the mesa, Gabe and Cougar fell in behind him, and Gabe leaned closer to Cougar, "That area yonder," he pointed across the valley, "up against the creek there might be a good place for a cabin."

Cougar was surprised at Gabe's remark, then twisted in her saddle to look at the area he indicated. Near the stream, the bright green of aspen fluttered in the breeze and the brilliant color of the hot springs pond showed in bright contrast. The tall ponderosa that climbed the steep slopes offered shade and refuge, but the shoulder that stood above the creek was where Gabe pointed, and Cougar smiled as she was reminded of their cabin in the Bitterroot foothills. It was upstream of where most of the village would be and offered a view of the chalk cliffs and the valley above and the flat lands below.

"It would be a good place. We will look at it after we make camp," answered Cougar, smiling.

Dusk was just lowering its curtain when the two families rode through the trees into the clearing on the shoulder above the creek. They stepped down, each one silent but looking about, thinking, considering, and as if they were given a cue, they started to speak at the same time. They laughed and Gabe said, "Go ahead, what do you think?" as he nodded to Cougar.

She smiled and walked toward the aspen that fronted the clearing, looked through the trees to the chalk cliffs beyond the valley bottom, and turned with a broad smile, "It is beautiful!"

Dove laughed and clapped, and the two women embraced. Gabe looked from the women to Ezra for his thoughts, "I like it! And there's plenty of trees nearby to build with."

Gabe nodded, grinning, looked at the others, "Then I guess we're home!"

ABOUT THE AUTHOR

Born and raised in Colorado into a family of ranchers and cow-boys, B.N. Rundell is the youngest of seven sons. Juggling bull riding, skiing, and high school, graduation was a launching pad for a hitch in the Army Paratroopers. After the army, he finished his college education in Springfield, MO, and together with his wife and growing family, entered the ministry as a Baptist preacher.

Together, B.N. and Dawn raised four girls that are now married and have made them proud grandparents. With many years as a successful pastor and educator, he retired from the ministry and followed in the footsteps of his entre-preneurial father and started a successful insurance agency, which is now in the hands of his trusted nephew. He has also been a successful audiobook narrator and has recorded many books for several award-winning authors. Now finally realizing his life-long dream, B.N. has turned his efforts to writing a variety of books, from children's picture books and young adult adventure books, to the historical fiction and western genres.